Molly Elliot Seawell

The Lively Adventures of Gavin Hamilton

Molly Elliot Seawell

The Lively Adventures of Gavin Hamilton

ISBN/EAN: 9783337179717

Printed in Europe, USA, Canada, Australia, Japan

Cover: Foto ©Andreas Hilbeck / pixelio.de

More available books at **www.hansebooks.com**

[Page 255]

"IT IS MY TURN NOW!" SHOUTED GAVIN

THE LIVELY ADVENTURES

OF

GAVIN HAMILTON

By

MOLLY ELLIOT SEAWELL

AUTHOR OF "THE ROCK OF THE LION"
"A VIRGINIA CAVALIER" ETC.

ILLUSTRATED

BY H. C. EDWARDS

NEW YORK AND LONDON
HARPER & BROTHERS PUBLISHERS
1900

NOTE

In this story, as in all the other stories for the young written by the author, few, or no liberties have been taken with history and chronology.

Molly Elliot Seawell

ILLUSTRATIONS

THE
LIVELY ADVENTURES
OF
GAVIN
HAMILTON
BY
MOLLY ELLIOT SEAWELL

THE LIVELY
ADVENTURES OF GAVIN HAMILTON

In Silesia, the autumn of 1757 was one of frightful cold, of icy winds, of sunless days, and freezing nights. The land, made desolate by the contending armies of the Empress Queen, Maria Theresa, and Frederick the Great, of Prussia, suffered still more from this bitter and premature winter. The miserable inhabitants, many of them houseless, died by thousands, of cold and starvation. The wretched remnant of cattle left them perished; the fields lay untilled, the mills were only piles of charred ruins, and desolation brooded over the land. War could add but little more to the miseries of this unfortunate region; but Frederick of Prussia and the lion-hearted Empress of Austria fought as fiercely as they had done sixteen years before when the Titanic com-

bat had first begun. Rosbach had been fought—
that terrible battle in which Frederick prevailed
against the Austrians, who were assisted by the
soldiers of France and the money of England.
The Austrians and French had, at first, attempted
an orderly retreat; but the piercing cold, the constant fall of snow, and the difficulties of subsist-
ence, had very much interfered with this. Their
object was to reach Prince Charles of Lorraine,
in northwest Silesia, and many small bodies of
troops succeeded in maintaining their organiza-
tion until they joined Prince Charles. Others
were not so fortunate; soldiers found themselves
without officers, and officers found themselves
without men. In this last case was Captain St.
Arnaud, of the French regiment of Dufour, a
young gentleman who had exchanged his commission in the King's Musketeers, the most royal
of all the royal guards, for a line regiment where
he could see service. It cannot be denied that this
decision on Captain St. Arnaud's part surprised
his world, for he was a curled darling among the
ladies, and the most superlative dandy in Paris.
And, wonderful to say, he still looked the superlative dandy on the afternoon of the coldest day
he ever felt in his life, amid the snowy wastes

of Silesia, when, after two weeks of starving and
running away from the Prussians, it looked as if
the inevitable hour had come. There was, yet,
not a speck upon his handsome uniform; his long,
light hair lay in curls upon his shoulders—he had
admired his own locks too much to cover them up
with a periwig; and his delicate, handsome face,
now gaunt and pale, was exquisitely shaven.
Clearly, starving did not agree with his constitu-
tion. His whole life before that campaign had
been spent in the courts and camps of kings, and
he had missed those hardening and fortifying in-
fluences which is Fate's rough way of benefiting
her favorites. But faint and weak and hopeless
as he seemed, his soul was still unconquered, and
his eyes looked bravely around upon the desolate
waste before him. The cold, already intense, was
becoming severer every hour. St. Arnaud, being
naturally of a reflective nature, which he hid under
a mask of the utmost levity, was thinking to himself, as he patted the neck of his lean and patient
horse, " The whole social order depends on the
mercury in the tube. At a certain point, varying
in different races, all distinctions are abolished.
If my general were here this moment, I would be
as good as he; for the best man would be he who

3

could keep up his circulation best. And if my orderly were here—bah! he could only deprive me of my last chance of living through this night by rubbing down my horse for me, which exercise would keep my blood in circulation and increase the poor beast's chances of carrying me through to the end." His piercing eyes had swept the view in front of him, but he almost jumped out of his saddle as a voice at his elbow said: "My Captain! I salute you!"

Close behind him, on a very good horse, sat a young private soldier of St. Arnaud's company. St. Arnaud at once recognized him; he was so tall, so fresh coloured, so well made that he attracted attention in the ranks; but private soldiers to St. Arnaud represented not names, but numbers. He thought this young fellow was 472 on the regimental roll, but had no idea of his name. He was a contrast to St. Arnaud in every way; for besides being a perfect picture of physical well-being, the young soldier was in rags. In one the inner man had suffered, in the other the outer man. Having spoken, the young man awaited speech from his officer with as much coolness as if he were on parade at Versailles, instead of being alone with him at nightfall in a frozen desert.

4

"I recognize you," said St. Arnaud, after a moment; "where are the others of your company?"

"I am the only man left, sir," replied the soldier; "as you know, we were very much cut up that villainous day at Rosbach; and when you were swept from us, in that last charge, we had already lost half our men. I don't know how it was, sir; certainly it was not the fault of our officers" —with another salute—"but I believe ours was the worst demoralized regiment in the French forces after Rosbach, and my company was the worst demoralized in the regiment. We had not an officer left above a corporal, but the handful of us could have remained together. Instead of doing that, it was *sauve qui peut* with all of us. Note, sir, I do not say we did not fight like devils at Rosbach; but being unused to defeat, we did not know how to take it. I cannot tell you how it is I come to be here alone; only I know that I, with twenty others, started out to make our way toward Prince Charles, and one by one the men dropped off, until yesterday morning, when, at sunrise, I found myself alone where I had bivouacked the night before with three comrades. They had gone off in the night, or early in the morning, to follow a road I did not believe would lead us where we wanted to go. I came this way, and well it was for me."

The young soldier's story, told jauntily, produced a singular effect on St. Arnaud. He had kept on hoping that, in spite of the accident of his being separated from his command—an accident caused by his own impetuosity carrying him too far in advance of his men—he would yet find his own personal command intact. But there was no more room for hope in the face of what was before his eyes and ringing in his ears. His countenance became so pale with grief and chagrin that he seemed about to drop from his saddle. He laid the reins on his horse's neck, and raised both arms above his head in a gesture of despair, but he said no word. The soldier, after waiting vainly for a question or an answer, spoke again.

"We have no time to lose, sir; we must cross this plain before night. I have some forage here and something in my haversack, and if we can get a fire we can live."

St. Arnaud, still silent, mechanically gathered up the reins again, and the horse instinctively made for a faint track beaten through the snow. The soldier followed, ten paces behind. On they travelled for an hour or two. As the sickly sun sank below the fringe of dun clouds in the west the cold became more terrible. A fierce wind set in, which drifted furious flurries of snow across the vast, white plain; and when the sky showed black against the white earth, neither man nor horse could travel farther. There was not a tree or even a bush in sight. They had passed a few dead horses on the dreary waste, but that was the only thing that broke the ghastly monotony of the way. Now they involuntarily halted, and each knew that from then until sunrise they would be fighting with the cold for life. The thought came back to St. Arnaud, who had scarcely spoken a word to his companion, how calamity levels all distinctions. It would not have surprised him in the least if, when he dismounted, and mechanically threw the reins to the soldier, to have heard him say: " Take care of your own horse, and I will attend to mine." Instead of this, the soldier only pointed to a little hillock near by, and said: " That place, sir, is a little sheltered from the wind. It will do us good to walk there."

St. Arnaud, whose faculties seemed frozen, obeyed the soldier. As he was tramping through the half darkness, his eyes blinded by the snow,

7

and the icy blast nearly cutting him to pieces, he heard a shout of joy behind him. The soldier had suddenly stumbled upon something which was worth to them at that moment all the gold in the Bank of France. It was nothing less than a broken gun-carriage, of which a few inches of the wheel appeared above the snow. The soldier dashed toward it, and tugged and pulled at it, shouting out exclamations of joy, as a man will who has found that which will give him life. St. Arnaud watched him dully as he wrenched such of it apart as he could, and dragging it to the sheltered spot under the hillock, where St. Arnaud held the trembling horses, scooped out a hole in the snow, and with a flint and steel struck a flash of fire.

At first, the flame flickered tamely; then, suddenly, it burst into a glory of light and warmth. St. Arnaud advanced, still leading the poor horses, who gazed at the flames with an intelligent joy, almost human.

By that time it was so black overhead and so white underfoot, and the swirling snow was so whipped about by the furious north wind, that it seemed as if the two men and the two shivering horses were alone in a universe of cold and snow and blackness. The young soldier first gave the horses the feed they had carried, and melting some snow in a tin pan he carried in his knapsack, gave them to drink. Then, washing out the pan, he produced some bacon and cheese and black bread. St. Arnaud showed the first sign of interest so far, by handing out his canteen, of which one whiff caused the young soldier's wide mouth to come open with a grin, that showed the whitest teeth imaginable. And then, huddling under their cloaks, officer and soldier shared their first meal together. That day month St. Arnaud had been entertained by a countess in one of the finest houses in Vienna, and the young soldier had fared sumptuously in the kitchen with the maids; but to-night they were supping together, and only too glad to sup at all. At last, all the bacon and cheese being devoured, St. Arnaud's spirit seemed to rouse from its torpor. He looked at the soldier attentively and asked:

" What is your name ? "

" Ameeltone," was the response.

St. Arnaud's French ear did not detect the strange pronunciation of the name, yet he could not quite make it out.

" Can you spell it ? " he asked.

" Oh, yes. H-a-m-i-l-t-o-n—Ameeltone."

9

"But that is English."

"Yes; my name is English all over. Gavin is my first name "—and he pronounced it Garvan.

"Have you any English blood in you?"

"I have not a drop of any but English blood, my Captain. My father, Sir Gavin Hamilton, is an Englishman; and my mother, God bless her, is Lady Hamilton."

"Then," said St. Arnaud, very naturally, "what are you doing as a trooper in Dufour's regiment?"

"Because," replied Gavin, taking up the tin pan and scooping out the last remnants of their supper, "my father is a great rascal." And he washed the pan out with snow.

St. Arnaud, accustomed to the extreme filial respect of the French for their parents, felt a shock at Gavin's cool characterization of his father, and said in reply:

"A man sometimes has cause for resentment against his father, but seldom calls him a rascal."

"True, my Captain," cheerfully replied Gavin, "but my father is a terrible rascal. He has ill-used my mother, the finest creature God ever made. What do you think of a man with a great fortune deserting his wife and child in a foreign land

and then using all his power to make her admit she
is not his wife, when he knows she is; and when
he finds she has a soul not to be terrified, trying
to fool her into a divorce? But I tell you, my Captain, my mother is a brave lady. She told him and
wrote him that she was his lawful wife, and that
she would defend me—I was a little boy then—
that she would have no divorce, lest it reflect on me,
and that no one of my rights would be bartered
away by her. And at that very time she could
barely keep body and soul together by giving lessons in Paris. She is well educated, luckily, being
an English officer's daughter. The English laws
are hard on poor and friendless women, and being
in France, too, my mother had little chance to
prove her rights. She looked to me, however, to
be able one day to maintain all she had claimed;
and she taught me carefully, so that, as she said,
when I came to the condition and estate of a gentleman, I might know how to bear myself. She
did not wish to go back to England, where she knew
persecution awaited her, and brought me up as
much an English boy as she could in France. The
only thing that troubled her was my pronunciation—she always laughs when I pronounce my own
name. I have an English way of using my fists

when I am angry. She scolds me, but I know her brothers fought like that when they were lads at school."

"How came you to join the army?"

"Faith, sir, I had no choice. The King's recruiting officers came after me, and I had to go. But I cannot say I regretted it, for I could never have been anything else but a soldier, and I have a better chance to rise in the army than in any of the humble callings open to me in civil life. My mother said it was best—that I came of good fighting stock on her side—her brothers were officers, and as far back as she knows her ancestors they were mostly in the army and navy."

The fire was burning brightly now; they were warmed through, their hunger was appeased, and so comfortable was their situation that they were both in a mood to entertain and be entertained. A fire in the snow and a supper of cheese and bacon meant luxury to St. Arnaud now, who had been brought up in palaces, and he found himself listening to Gavin's story with the same interest that the Arab in the parching desert listens to the story-teller who makes him forget all his miseries.

"Did you ever see your father?" he asked.

"Once. My father was sent to the court of the

12

Empress Queen on a diplomatic mission. He passed secretly through Paris and sent for me. I went with the sole idea that he might do justice to my mother. But I might have saved my shoe leather. However, what I did that day to my father is written to my credit in heaven's books, for I mauled him well, and I was but eighteen— I am only nineteen now."

St. Arnaud could not refrain from a look of disapproval, and Gavin, noting it, asked at once, with the greatest *naïveté:*

" But he spoke abominably of my mother, and any man who speaks one disrespectful word of her —he is my enemy, and I am his. Would not you do the same by your mother ? "

And St. Arnaud involuntarily answered " Yes."

" Well, then," continued Gavin, rising to his feet, " are you surprised that I should think I did a righteous act in flying at Sir Gavin ? He is a strong, well-made man, though not so big as I am now, and as I took him by surprise, I succeeded in knocking him off his chair before he had got out half he had meant to say about my mother. His valet came running in then, and Sir Gavin, smiling as he wiped some blood off his face. sent the man away. Oh, he was a cool one! He smiled all the time we were together, and he laughed aloud when I called myself Gavin Hamilton.

" ' Garvan Ameeltone! ' he cried, mocking me."

Gavin was now thoroughly inspired by his own eloquence. He stood up and put his hands behind his back, English fashion, while repeating his father's words and mimicking him in an odd, drawling voice. St. Arnaud fully believed in the scene that Gavin not only told, but acted before him. Even the two horses, tethered close to the red circle of light, lifted their heads, attracted by the ringing human voice, and seemed to be listening attentively to the story of Gavin Hamilton's wrongs and revenges.

"My father then, instead of being angry with me, seemed to like me the better, and offered me everything—everything if I would abandon my mother. He would acknowledge me as his son, according to both the French and English law, for I was born in France; he would promise never to marry again, and I don't know what else beside. It was then my turn to laugh. I said: ' Wait until I am twenty-one, and then see if I do not prove I am your son. And as for marrying again, you dare not in my mother's lifetime.'

14

"There was an hour-glass in the room, and Sir Gavin said to me: 'In about twenty minutes all the sand will have run out of that glass. I give you until then to accept my offer.' For answer I smashed the hour-glass on the hearth. It was then he spoke insultingly of my mother, and it was then that I think I laid up treasures in heaven by the way I pounded him. I got several good blows at him before that rascal of a valet came in and pulled me off."

The wind was howling so, and the gusts of snow so driven between them, that St. Arnaud drew close to Gavin to hear the rest of the story. Gavin, who was thoroughly enjoying the recital of his affair, stopped long enough to throw some of the iron work of the gun-carriage into the fire, when it speedily grew red hot, and glowed radiantly, adding materially to the warmth. He then resumed, in response to the interest plain in St. Arnaud's face:

"I trudged back to our garret, where my mother was waiting for me. It was a cold evening, and my mother had a little fire for me—fuel is cruelly dear in Paris, isn't it, my Captain?—and she also had something for me to eat. She let me be warmed and filled before asking me any questions, for my mother has that English coolness which nothing seems able to disturb. When I was through eating I told her about the interview. I told her all except the words Sir Gavin had used about her, but I said they were such as no man, father or no father, should speak of her without being made to suffer all I could make him suffer for it. Then my mother suddenly burst into tears, and taking my face between her hands, kissed me, and said some of those sweet things that women say to those they love; and I replied: ' What matters it about his threats and promises? You are his wife; I am his son and heir. Wait until I am twenty-one, and I will go to England and proclaim it all. If Sir Gavin Hamilton deals with us thinking he is dealing with a helpless woman and a boy, he will find we are not quite so helpless as he fancies we are. The notion that I, within three years of my majority, would make a bargain with him! It is absurd!' "

" Quite so," replied St. Arnaud, " and his anxiety to make a bargain with you shows that he knows you will have to be reckoned with."

Then, drawing his watch from his pocket, he said: " We must divide the watch to-night. I will take the first hour until one in the morning. The fire will last the night, and rubbing the horses down will warm us up."

Gavin then discovered that St. Arnaud meant the distinction between officer and private to be overlooked. They both went to work on their horses, and for fifteen minutes nothing more was said. Gavin had a small supply of forage, and he noticed that St. Arnaud had a large haversack strapped to his saddle. Gavin hoped that it was something to sustain life in man or beast; but presently, both having got through with their horses, St. Arnaud, noticing for the first time Gavin's tattered clothes, said:

"You are ill-clad for such weather as this. Yonder in my haversack is a second uniform, which you may have. You see, I am not used to running away, and carried with me clothes, when I should have taken food."

Gavin's eyes sparkled. He fetched the haversack, and tore it open. A change of delicate linen, some toilet articles, and a handsome new uniform tumbled out. Gavin was in ecstasy when he saw the uniform.

"Oh, my Captain," he cried, "do you mean this for me? I have longed—yes, longed to wear an officer's uniform; and I have a presentiment that

17

2

if I once take off a private soldier's coarse clothes, I shall never again wear them."

And as quick as lightning he slipped off his rags, jumped into the uniform, and then, in the excess of his delight, he gave three loud and ear-piercing huzzas, that were half lost in the tumult of the wind. At the same moment he threw his own tattered clothes as far as he could swing them, the wind seizing and scattering them; next, he dashed away the dragoon's sabre which he carried.

"There you go," he shouted; "you never were any good as a weapon, and I will replace you by an officer's sword with a gold handle. And meanwhile I will defend myself with my horse-pistol!"

St. Arnaud laughed until the tears came into his eyes. He had not in a month been so amused and interested as in this young man, so strangely found, and to whom he owed his life by the finding him. Gavin looked a little sheepish at St. Arnaud's laughter, but was compensated by his next words.

"You are a fine-looking fellow, and you have the bearing of an officer. Why is it I never recognized you in the regiment?"

"I can't say. I only know it was not because

GAVIN THROWS AWAY HIS TROOPER'S SABRE

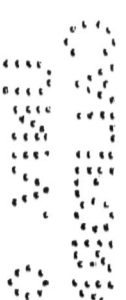

I did not want to be recognized. But I knew you, my Captain, and often looked at you as you stepped along so elegant, so debonair, with such beautiful cambric handkerchiefs, and such small polished boots. I heard, too, that your quarters were like a lady's boudoir, and you had a private wagon to carry your clavier and *viol da gamba!*"

"Yes," replied St. Arnaud, somewhat ruefully. "I shall know better in my next campaign."

Gavin, then rolling himself in his blanket, lay down before the fire. By its red light his dark, upturned eyes could be seen, and they were full of hope and even joy. Defeat and disaster were lightly taken by this young soldier. In a little while, though, he was sleeping, with the soft, low breathing of a baby.

Beyond the red circle of the fire all was blackness, and, except the roaring of the wind, all was silence. A few stars flickered dimly in the cold heavens above them, but they were often obscured by the flurries of snow. St. Arnaud sat still in front of the fire, for it was not yet necessary to walk up and down to keep alive. His face was pale and impassive, and he was still suffering from the shock of flight and defeat. It seemed to him as if a hundred years separated him from the year before, or even the month before. The hours dragged by toward midnight. Every moment it grew colder, but the fire still lasted. At last, at one o'clock, St. Arnaud waked Gavin, who rose instantly. St. Arnaud showed him a pocket thermometer, with the mercury down to zero.

"That's nothing," cried Gavin jauntily. "I will throw some of the iron of the gun-carriage on the fire, and if I see you freezing, I will wake you up, never fear."

St. Arnaud lay down and, covered with Gavin's blanket, soon fell asleep. Gavin watched him all the time, thinking:

"Some men in my place would think themselves unfortunate at this moment. I don't. This is my first real stroke of fortune. I have an officer's uniform—*parbleu!* what may I not expect in the way of good luck!"

Absorbed in a delicious dream of the future, the rest of the night seemed short to Gavin. A ghastly half light succeeded the darkness; and then all at once a pale rose colour appeared in the eastern sky, and a faint golden haze overspread the snow-covered earth. The distant mountains glowed in an opaline light—it was the dawn of a cloudless winter day.

Gavin, however, beyond the thrill which morning brings to men of his youth and type, noticed
nothing, being occupied with the horses, and with
the preparation of the last of his cheese and bacon
in the tin pan. When it was ready he waked St.
Arnaud, who was sleeping soundly.

"Come, my Captain," he called out. "We are
both alive. There is something to eat. The
weather is fair, and the sun is rising. And faith!
I feel as if I would like to right about face and
go back to fighting those confounded Prussians
again."

St. Arnaud got up instantly. In fifteen minutes
they had finished all they had to eat, had mounted,
and were travelling along the faint track in the
snow which indicated the highroad. As they
turned their horses' heads, St. Arnaud said to
Gavin:

"Ride by me." And Gavin, without the least
impertinence, replied firmly:

"I meant to. No man in an officer's uniform
rides behind his captain."

CHAPTER II

St. Arnaud and Gavin travelled all that day
through a scene of desolation, but the sun shone,
and they were approaching a part of the country
where at least food could be had, and their circumstances seemed so much improved, that all at once
the world took on an altogether different aspect.
No man could long endure, and live, the hideous
depression from which St. Arnaud had suffered
since Rosbach; and when his soul made a final
rally, it was to perch upon heights of hope and
joy. He felt sure they would beat Frederick of
Prussia, and one short month would see a revival
of the fortunes of the Empress Queen. He so expressed himself to Gavin, who had never suffered
any depression whatever. And each found a source
of vivid interest in the other's personality. St.
Arnaud had never met a man in the least like this
young French-Englishman, and the story of the
mother, the woman who was Lady Hamilton by
right, starving and freezing with her. child, but

always working in her miserable attic in a great foreign city, was moving to him. He saw that the son of such a mother would be of tough fibre. As for Gavin, St. Arnaud's beauty, grace, and superior knowledge of the world were so captivating, that the riding by his side in an officer's uniform was an intoxicating pleasure.

"Often," thought Gavin to himself, looking sidewise at St. Arnaud's clear and handsome profile, " have I watched you at parade, and longed— oh, how I have longed—to be on equal terms with you. I shall be yet, because I am resolved, if a man has any share in his own destiny, to be one day a sublieutenant; and then—pouf! the rest is easy." He would have dearly liked to ask St. Arnaud questions, but he remembered that, although they rode side by side, he was still a private soldier. St. Arnaud, however, took the privilege of an officer, and questioned Gavin freely.

" Can you read and write? " he asked.

" Like a notary," replied Gavin promptly. " My mother took good care to give me an excellent English education herself, and she was well qualified, too. Often has she taught me out of her head when she would be working at her needle for a living, for to that has Sir Gavin Hamilton reduced my mother; and he wanted me to go home and live with him—may the devil take him now and forever! My mother taught me also a little Latin, a little Spanish, and I myself learned a good deal of German from those Austrian allies of ours."

"You far excel me," responded St. Arnaud, " and yet I had the best teachers in France."

At which Gavin replied proudly: " I can ask for wine in four languages."

" I only wish you had a chance to ask for it in one—to make signs, for that matter."

They rode on in silence for a few moments, when Gavin spoke again.

" My Captain," he said in a coaxing voice, " I have something to ask of you—a favour—such a favour as a man asks but once in a lifetime."

" Considering that my meeting you last night saved my life, I should feel a little awkward in refusing you anything I could grant."

" It is this, then. You see, I have on this uniform. As long as I wear it the world thinks me an officer. Let me wear it, and let me dream myself a lieutenant until we reach the army of Prince Charles! Our regiment is scattered; it may never be reorganized; and as soon as we join

24

Prince Charles there will be fighting, and what glorious chances has a soldier then! Give me but one chance under fire, and I promise you I will come out of it so that I will be made an officer in truth."

St. Arnaud stopped, amazed at Gavin's presumption; but one look at his face, his eyes glowing with furious entreaty, checked the peremptory refusal upon his lips. Instead he said:

" You will be discovered."

" Certainly; but a general who discovers a private soldier, by birth a gentleman, who is known to be brave and loyal—for that I am, and challenge any man to say nay—wishing and deserving to be an officer, will make him one. The French army is not like the Austrian, or even these pigs of Prussians."

"You will discover yourself—betray yourself, in short, in whatever society you find yourself. No one will take you for an officer."

" I think I told you I was the son of Lady Hamilton," responded Gavin coldly.

St. Arnaud hesitated for a moment or two; then, with a brilliant smile, holding out his hand to Gavin, he said:

" Every word I have spoken was against the

impulse of my heart. You are an officer now, as far as I can make you; and trust me, when we reach Prince Charles, he shall hear your story first from me."

Gavin, who was usually glib of speech, became silent under the influence of strong emotion. He only held St. Arnaud's hand in a grip that was like steel. Presently releasing it, he said:

" My life is yours—I have nothing more now to offer." Then, suddenly recovering himself, he cried joyfully: " Oh, that my mother could see me now! It fretted her proud soul to see me a private soldier, but she said no word. And if I only remember all she told me, I will prove myself a gentleman. She was, as I told you last night, always preparing me for something higher. She made me learn English table manners even when we had precious little to eat. And wash! Those English are mad about soap and water. My mother has washed me when I was a little lad until I shrieked for mercy; but scrub, wash, wash, scrub, every day, and twice a day. Illness, cold, nothing excused me from that infernal tub. But at last I got to like it; and now I like cold water as well as any whale that swims the Arctic seas. Here is the proof."

Gavin produced with great pride a small, round lump tied with strings, and on the strings being cut, it expanded into a huge sponge.

" And this—and this—and this—" he added, handing out some coarse soap, a comb, and a razor.

For reply, St. Arnaud produced not only a sponge, but a small towel, a cake of scented soap, a silver comb, and a pearl-handled razor. Gavin's eyes gleamed. " These will I have when I am an officer ! " he cried.

They resumed their way. The joy that shone in Gavin's face was contagious. St. Arnaud smiled at the thought that a suit of clothes and the hope of a sublieutenancy could give so much happiness to any one ; but he did not know that it meant all which the young soldier coveted in life.

That day they entered a tract of country where an occasional house still stood; and they even found an inn, soon after midday, where they got a coarse but abundant meal. After that the aspect of the country steadily improved, and in the early winter dusk they found themselves approaching a comfortable country mansion with pleasure grounds around it. The windows were tightly barred, but smoke was pouring from one of the chimneys.

"Now, my young sublieutenant," cried St. Arnaud, laughing, "we will find gentlepeople in this pleasant bivouac; and, remember, you are an officer. Don't call me 'my Captain,' and whatever you do, don't show any subservience to me. Contradict me occasionally, and when I say it is a certain time by my watch, say my watch is fast or slow—anything to show we are on an equality."

"I will remember," answered Gavin gravely.

Dismounting before the door, Gavin began a rat-tat-tat which sounded like an earthquake. There was no response, and after banging at the door for five minutes he walked around the corner of the house. There was a door leading into the kitchen quarters, but it, too, was closely fastened. The cold was becoming intense, and Gavin was about to return to St. Arnaud and discuss the propriety of breaking a window, when a man-servant appeared upon the scene. He did not observe Gavin in the half darkness, and, on hearing the heavy clump of the rustic's shoes, the kitchen door opened an inch or two, and a maid, with a foolish, frightened face, whispered:

"Get the other one to help you with the wood-basket; we must have the wood in the house at once. But be quiet about it, for there has been a great pounding at the front door, and we don't wish to let any one in."

Gavin then noticed a great, two-handled basket piled with wood such as the huge stoves of the region required. The man went off to get help in lifting it, and an idea jumped into Gavin's mind. " I'll get in the house and open the door for St. Arnaud," thought he; and as soon as the man's back was turned he went to the basket, softly removed some of the wood, crawled in, and, artistically arranging a few sticks so as to conceal himself, waited some minutes. Then the servant, with another one, approached; a stout pole was run between the two handles, and the basket, with Gavin and the logs, was picked up, carried through the kitchen, then into a long corridor, and finally to the main entrance hall, where there was a vast porcelain stove. At that moment Gavin heard a light step descending the stairs, and an exquisitely sweet voice say:

" How can you let those poor creatures outside suffer in this cold? I order you to open the door immediately."

" But, madame," said the maid, who had fol-lowed, " we had express orders from the master and mistress to let no one in."

At this moment the basket was let down, and in another instant Gavin, having disengaged himself with quiet dexterity from the wood, stepped out of the basket, and making his best bow, said in his best German: " Madame, I will obey your orders, if these louts will not," and running to the door, drew the bolt, and in walked Captain St. Arnaud.

The two men-servants gaped in grotesque horror at the load they had brought in; the maid began to scream violently; only the lady retained her self-possession.

" To whom am I indebted," she asked of Gavin with perfect composure, " for carrying out my orders with such unexpected promptness? "

" To Sublieutenant Gavin Hamilton, of Dufour's regiment of dragoons, in the service of His Majesty of France," replied Gavin with equal coolness, saying to himself meanwhile, " Aha! St. Arnaud will see that I have the composure of a gentleman." Then he said, " Permit me, madame, to present Captain St. Arnaud of my regiment."

St. Arnaud bowed with the utmost gravity, although immensely tickled at Gavin, and the three gentlepeople stood entirely at ease, while the three servants were completely disconcerted.

"I am Madame Ziska," said the lady of the charming voice, speaking in French. "I am running away from the Prussians toward Vienna. This house belongs to acquaintances of mine, who have left it. The servants in charge, knowing me, gave me permission to remain the night here; and although I had no authority to let any one else in, I certainly should have opened the door had not Lieutenant Hamilton done so for me."

Neither cold nor hunger nor flight had dulled either St. Arnaud's or Gavin's appreciation of beauty and charm. There was no great beauty in Madame Ziska, but an exquisite grace of bearing, a face full of expression, and a beautiful figure. She was one of those women whose age it was impossible to tell. She was, in truth, thirty, but she might have been twenty-five or thirty-five. Nor was her nationality apparent either in her appearance or her language, for her French was immaculate; and neither St. Arnaud nor Gavin Hamilton knew enough of the German language to judge of how she spoke it when she addressed the servants. St. Arnaud thought first of the poor beasts outside, and said to the men-servants: "Have our horses attended to at once, and look for either money or kicks, according to how you do it."

The two men disappeared, and the maid, apparently profiting by the suggestion of money, said very respectfully:

" Supper is not yet ready, madame; and I will add something for these gentlemen," and disappeared.

Madame Ziska then led the way to a small sitting-room, where a stove glowed, candles gleamed, and a table was set with linen and plate. She seated herself before the stove, and not until then did St. Arnaud and Gavin proceed to warm their chilled bodies. St. Arnaud watched Gavin closely, but with amusement, as if he were assisting at the first production of a new comedy, when he saw this young private soldier of nineteen masquerading as a gentleman. Gavin himself saw the joke, and St. Arnaud could not refrain from bursting out laughing when Gavin, surveying himself coolly in a mirror on the wall, remarked:

" Madame, I am indebted to my brother officer for these clothes—it is quite a story—and, *sacre!* I hardly know myself in this rig."

" But," thought St. Arnaud, " wait until supper is served. The table is a place to tell a man's up-bringing."

The door opened, and the servants entered,

bringing with them a very good supper. Gavin
rose instantly, and forestalled St. Arnaud in placing a chair for Madame Ziska, at which the captain's heretofore smiling face assumed a scowl.
There is such a thing as learning a lesson too well
and too promptly. They seated themselves, and
a very jolly supper party they made. Madame
Ziska's conversation proved as charming as her
appearance. She talked with the utmost ease and
apparent frankness, but of her own condition in
life she said not a word. Yet, there was something convincingly honest about her; and St. Arnaud, who knew the world thoroughly, felt as much
confidence in her as did the unsophisticated Gavin.
He shrewdly suspected her to be a professional
artist of some description, who possessed, by some
chance, a higher degree of education and breeding
than was usual in those times. He treated her,
however, as if she had been a princess in her own
right, and Madame Ziska accepted it with perfect
dignity, as her just due.

Gavin had never before sat at table with an officer, and he watched St. Arnaud quite as closely as '
St. Arnaud watched him. He carried off his part
wonderfully well, but it was not quite perfection.
He laughed and talked too much, airing his senti-

ments in the four languages he claimed to know,
which, except English and French, he spoke very
ungrammatically. St. Arnaud, pleasant but criti-
cal, noticed all, while Madame Ziska's sweet, in-
scrutable smile revealed nothing. There was a
harpsichord in the room, and as soon as they had
finished supper St. Arnaud jumped up and, opening it, burst into a sentimental song, accompanying
himself brilliantly. This was too much for Gavin,
who was so charmed that he altogether forgot the
part he was playing, and also the training his
mother had given him, and acted as he would at a
bivouac when a comrade sang a good song. In the
excess of his enjoyment he sat down on the floor,
close to the glowing stove, and after a while established himself comfortably at full length, his head
resting on his elbows, which he dug into the carpet.
St. Arnaud saw it all out of the tail of his eye, until
Gavin, suddenly catching St. Arnaud's amused
glance fixed on him, jumped up, red and embar-
rassed.

" That is for not remembering what my mother
told me," he thought, with the deepest vexation.
" However," he reflected again, " I shall soon overcome the demoralization of camp manners in company like this," and he demurely seated himself on

a sofa. The song closed in a beautiful cadenza, but it was drowned in a tremendous tramping of hoofs, and the maid-servants rushed in, bawling: " The Prussians! The Prussians! "

St. Arnaud's and Gavin's first sensation was one of stupid surprise. They had not thought a Prussian to be within fifty miles. Madame Ziska, however, showed not an instant's discomposure. She at once opened the door of a closet in the room, saying, " It is strategy, not rashness, which is wanted now; " and almost pushing them in, she took the key out of the lock, and passed it to them in the inside. Then, seating herself nonchalantly, she trimmed the candles and took up a book to read.

It was so quickly done that neither St. Arnaud nor Gavin had a connected thought until they found themselves in the closet, nor could they recall which one locked the door. They gazed stupidly at each other in the half light which filtered through the glass doors lined with green silk; and then they found that, although concealed from sight themselves, they could yet see any one in the room through little holes in the moth-eaten silk behind the glass.

The sound of many feet entering the house was now heard, and in a moment more the door was opened, and a Prussian officer ushered in, a short, slender man, wearing a shabby surtout and nondescript uniform. Several other officers followed; but from the moment the short, slender man entered, neither one of the prisoners in the closet, nor had Madame Ziska, eyes for any one but him.

His face was wan and weather-beaten, his nose high and prominent, and his brow and mouth rather unpleasing. But his gray-blue eyes redeemed an otherwise sinister face. They were exquisitely clear, soft yet sparkling, and their mild expression flatly contradicted the hardness and even cruelty of his other features.

He advanced to the stove, slightly and negligently saluting Madame Ziska, who rose and bowed. As he addressed no word to her, after standing a moment she quietly reseated herself. The other officers remained standing, and a shiver seemed to run through them at Madame Ziska's action. The man in the nondescript uniform noticed it, and smiled faintly. He sat down, warmed his hands at the stove, while the officers stood rigidly at attention. Madame Ziska read diligently, and St. Arnaud and Gavin in the closet scarcely dared to breathe.

After five minutes of this the shabby man looked

around him, made a slight motion with his hand, and every officer, saluting, filed out of the door, and he was left alone with Madame Ziska.

Madame Ziska continued to read. Presently the strange personage spoke to her in French, and in the clearest and sweetest voice imaginable.

" You have a great deal of *sang froid,* madame."

" One needs it in this bustling world," replied Madame Ziska calmly, withdrawing her eyes for a moment from her book.

" Ahem ! " A pause. " Your French is very good."

" So is yours, monsieur."

" It is the only language, after all."

" You must be well up in the graces of His Majesty, the King of Prussia, who loves everything French, although he fights France."

" Well, yes. You think me a major, or a colonel, perhaps, in the King's body-guard."

" Majors and colonels do not have the staff that came with you into this room just now. You are a general at least."

" No. Higher."

" A field-marshal ? "

" Higher still."

" Prince Henry of Prussia ? "

37

" Prince Henry rises when I speak to him."

Madame Ziska rose and made him a profound courtesy.

" Sire, you are the King of Prussia."

CHAPTER III

At the announcement that the shabby man with the sparkling and speaking eyes and the soft and melodious voice was Frederick of Prussia, the greatest captain of the age, the two men concealed in the closet grew rigid with astonishment. They did not need his careless, but confirmatory nod to be convinced of his identity; but when he spoke it was to say:

"Yes, I am the King of Prussia. A great many people know me by sight—more do not. You are evidently one of the latter class."

Madame Ziska remained standing respectfully, and answered Frederick's last speech by saying:

"Your Majesty will not think me a flatterer when I say I knew from the moment you entered this room that you were no ordinary man."

"And I knew," said Frederick, with a faint smile, which transfigured his whole face, "that you were no ordinary woman when you faced half a dozen strange men as you did. I should like to

39

have a regiment of men as cool as you are. How they would stand fire! Pray be seated. War is a tiresome business," he continued, after Madame Ziska had resumed her chair. " But it is my trade, and a man must work at his trade. However, I like my tools—my soldiers." Then, throwing himself back in his chair, he kept on, as if merely thinking aloud. "I am like the bourgeois— of whom I have no great opinion—I am absorbed in my trade. Time was when I had tastes; now 'tis nothing but whether I can beat Prince Charles as I did Marshal Soubise the other day. I like the work less as time goes on; but I like other things less still."

" You still like music, your Majesty."

" How do you know that ? "

Madame Ziska rose, and stepping lightly up to him, with the utmost grace and quickness drew the pieces of a flute out of the pocket of his surtout, and deftly screwed them together, evidently knowing all about it. Then, putting the flute to her rosy lips, she played a little French air, to which Frederick listened enraptured.

" Ah ! " he cried; " that carries me back to my peaceful days at Ruppin, when my flute was my only company for days together."

Madame Ziska, seeing that she had found something in which he was interested, went to the harpsichord, and seating herself, sang a French song in
a sweet, agreeable voice.

Frederick was charmed.

"Madame, have you any other accomplishments?" he cried. "I have not sunk so far into
the savage as I thought, if music can still give me
such pleasure."

Madame Ziska hesitated, a roguish smile playing
over her face.

"Did your Majesty say you played the little air
I tried just now on the flute?"

"Yes, yes. My sister, the Margravine of Bai-
reuth, first taught it to me, and accompanied me
on the harpsichord."

He seized the flute and began playing, and Madame Ziska, with the greatest coolness in the world,
picking up her skirts, executed a *pas de seul* that
was a wonder of skill and grace. The intricacy
of her steps was marvellous; she sprung into the
air and alighted on the point of her toe, and then
spun around with dazzling dexterity; her arms,
used with exquisite effect, seemed to have the
power of wings to support her; but when, with a
final bound and a sinking to the floor, and rising

with consummate grace, she was about to conclude
her dance, a knock came at the door. Madame
Ziska, with lightning quickness, seated herself demurely, while the King, not to be behindhand, put
his flute behind him, and called out petulantly:

"Come in."

An officer entered and, saluting, said:

"Did your Majesty call?"

"No," tartly responded the King. "Did you
not hear me playing on my flute? A man must
have some recreation, and because I do not puff
smoke by the hour, nor gamble, nor make a beast
of myself with wine, I am not thereby without
tastes."

The officer was so taken aback by this onslaught
that he hastily closed the door.

The effect of Madame Ziska's dance was not less
electrifying to the two men in the closet than on the
King. St. Arnaud was somewhat surprised, but
Gavin's eyes were nearly starting out of his head,
and St. Arnaud could scarcely keep from laughing,
although a laugh then would have cost him his life.

"There, madame!" said Frederick, when the
officer had hastily shut the door. "You see one
of the disadvantages of my calling. It would not
surprise my military family in the least if I were

to be guilty of crimes and call them amusements;
but that I should occasionally play the flute never
fails to astonish them. Bah! But tell me this,"
he resumed, as Madame Ziska, panting after her
exercise, fanned herself. "How comes it that a
woman who dances in a manner worthy of the
Grand Opera at Paris should speak so well? Pardon my bluntness; I have fallen into it, because the
women I see are chiefly court ladies who never
would have done talking, when once they begun, if
I did not use a little *brusquerie* with them occasionally."

Madame Ziska laughed a singularly pleasant
and honest laugh. "I do myself not know," she
replied, "except that as soon as I learned to read
I wished to put it to practice. I come of the very
bourgeoisie you were abusing just now; but circumstances placed me with a certain person in particular who was above me in station and highly educated, and, naturally, I strove to raise myself to a
higher level than a mere dancer."

"Humph! Where are you going now?"

"I am on my way to Vienna. Your Majesty has
fluted so to the Austrians and French that they are
always dancing—but not of my kind. And I am
going where I can find people who will think of

43

some one else than your Majesty long enough to let a poor artist make a living."

"You may see the Empress Queen at Vienna, but not exactly as you see me—ha! ha! However, I will give you some tangible proof that you have seen me."

He fumbled in his pockets and brought out a plain silver snuff-box with the royal cipher on it. Then taking a penknife from his pocket, he scratched on the lid, " Frédéric," adding: " I, and only I, so write my name."

Madame Ziska's conduct on receiving this was quite different from what might have been expected from her previous debonair behaviour. Her eyes filled with tears, and she clasped her hands in gratitude.

Within the closet, St. Arnaud and Gavin remained breathless and noiseless as they thought. But those clear, limpid eyes of Frederick's saw more than was apparent. He rose and, carelessly approaching the door, raised the hilt of his sword, and bringing it down with a thundering crash, the glass door was shivered, the green silk torn apart, and the two French officers stood revealed.

Gavin Hamilton thought afterward: " There is something in being trained as an officer, after all," for, although as brave a man as St. Arnaud, he involuntarily shrunk back into the closet when discovered; but St. Arnaud, deliberately stepping out, bowed to the ground and said with the utmost suavity:

"Thanks, your Majesty. It *was* warm in there; but we did not think of breaking the glass for air!"

At this Frederick burst into a hearty laugh; the coolness of St. Arnaud amused him. Madame Ziska turned pale, but at the King's ringing laugh she recovered herself, and said, smiling roguishly:

"We are three to one, but we will spare your Majesty!"

Frederick laughed again at this, and seeing Gavin still trying to make himself small against the wall of the closet, the King leant in, and taking him by the collar, dragged him out, Gavin looking very sheepish and blushing furiously. And then the great King and the French officer, the private soldier and the dancer all laughed together.

"Madame and messieurs," cried Frederick, "you may claim each to have conferred a great favour on the King of Prussia; for I tell you I have not laughed so heartily this year. I thought I had forgotten how. Nor did I ever take a prisoner before with my own hand; and, gentlemen, each one of you is more than a match for me, and a younger man beside."

"Your Majesty has reason to boast of your prowess," returned St. Arnaud, while Gavin, suddenly remembering that he must act up to his character as an officer, said with the utmost naturalness:

"Sire, if only I had kept my wits about me, I would have knocked your Majesty down and jumped out of the window. But I never spoke with a king before, and I was so taken aback—faith! a baby might have captured me."

"Don't try the window, my fine fellow," said Frederick gayly, but with a warning note in his voice; "you do not suppose I am here without any escort? The fact is, however, I did not think there was a Frenchman or an Austrian in a hundred miles. What is your name and rank?" to St. Arnaud.

"Captain St. Arnaud, of the regiment of Dufour, and this is Sublieutenant Hamilton" (which he pronounced no better than Gavin) "of my regiment. We have been running away from you ever since Rosbach, and now, presto! you catch us like a couple of chickens in a barnyard."

46

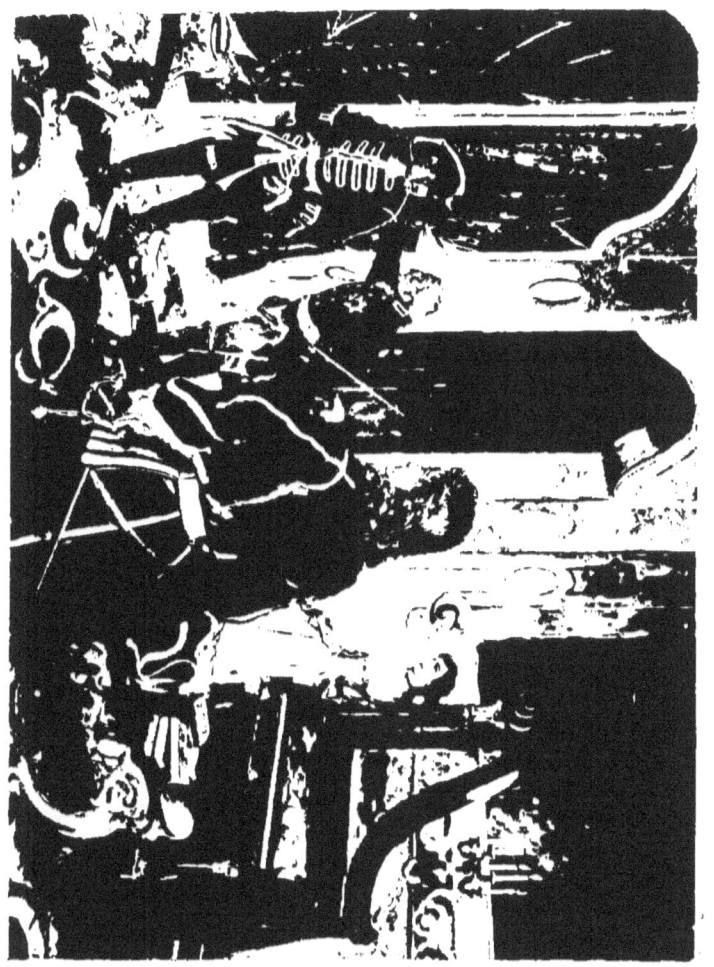

THE KING DRAGGED GAVIN OUT OF THE CLOSET

"And I broke up your little evening party with this lady. I suspected her of being a spy, but she charmed me so with her music and dancing that I forgot to ask her a word, and gave her the only thing of value I had about me—my snuff-box. But I must let my staff know that, single-handed, I captured a couple of tall Frenchmen." Then calling loudly in his clear, musical voice "Steiner!" a young officer opened the door as quickly as if he had sprung from the ground. When he saw St. Arnaud and Gavin he started with amazement.

"Taken with my own hand," said Frederick with a wave of his arm. "My compliments to the chief and the other gentlemen of my staff, and say I will not rejoin them to-night, but I shall be ready to start at daylight in the morning, and to keep a good lookout. There may be more than two Frenchmen about. You, Steiner, I will have to attend me; and keep the others well off in the other part of the house. We may have a little music while the rest are having their pipes and beer. And bring my writing-desk with you; I shall have work to do presently."

Steiner disappeared, and Madame Ziska, St. Arnaud, and Gavin, as if realizing that they were in the presence of the greatest king of his age, remained silent and standing.

"Pray be seated," said Frederick, with the charming manner he possessed, but did not always use. "It is not often I have either leisure or pleasure—the business of being a king requires a man to work like a galley-slave—but to-night I will indulge myself. I will imagine myself as I was twenty years ago, when, so far from fighting the French, I loved all that was French. Come, Madame, one more song."

Madame Ziska rose, and going to the harpsichord, sang a little French chansonnette. Frederick seemed delighted with it. As he truly said, it was as if he had gone back twenty years, when music and literature made up his life, and the future great captain was the gentle and studious Crown Prince.

"And _he_ sings," said Madame Ziska, pointing to St. Arnaud as she rose.

In obedience to a look from Frederick, St. Arnaud went to the harpsichord and sang; and then it was Steiner's turn, who roared out a German drinking song. Unlike the rest, Steiner was not at his ease before his King, although he tried hard to assume the air of unembarrassed gayety which

prevailed among the rest. But it was not a great
success. He knew the King too well to suppose
that the graceful abandon of an evening spent in
unexpectedly novel and agreeable company was a
fair sample of his usual moods and methods. The
rest, though, naturally pleased themselves with the
notion that they would be extremely favoured by
the King. Madame Ziska had already received
a valuable mark of his good-will in the silver snuff-
box, and expected to be sent rejoicing upon her
journey. Gavin's visions were so brilliant that he
almost came to regard their capture as a lucky accident. He kept thinking to himself: " Yesterday
I was a private soldier. To-night I sit with a
king. Surely, that means a turn of good fortune."

St. Arnaud, who knew more of kings than any
of them, was not so sanguine, but even he would
rather have been taken prisoner by Frederick than
any other man in the Prussian army.

The evening passed delightfully. Frederick
seemed to return to his early love for the French,
and nothing could exceed the grace of his allusions
to " my brother of France," French literature, art,
and all that pertained to them. The extent and
variety of his information were extraordinary, and
the charm of his voice and manner could not have

been excelled. Gavin had the good sense to remain in the background; Madame Ziska's manner, of respect, without obsequiousness, was as perfect as St. Arnaud's, who had learned many things at courts. At last one o'clock came. The King, looking at his watch, rose, and Madame Ziska, immediately taking the hint, left the room. The King said: "It is time to go to work," and Steiner picked up the writing-desk and prepared to move. "The worst of pleasant things is their ending. This room is yours, gentlemen, for the night; and, as you see, you will have company outside the window and in the corridors. And I am prepared to accept your parole."

An awkward silence ensued. Both Gavin and St. Arnaud remembered at the same moment that Gavin, not being an officer, was not entitled to his parole; while there were so few Prussian officers, if any, in the hands of the French, that St. Arnaud's exchange would be a matter of time and difficulty. After a moment he said, with a profound bow:

"I am much indebted to your Majesty, but I prefer to take my chances as a prisoner of war."

Gavin, who had determined to do as St. Arnaud did, bowed and said:

"Sire, so do I."

Frederick scowled—kings are easily offended, even when they play at Haroun al-Raschid—and then said coldly:

"I shall then refer you to my chief of staff. I am under obligations to you for a pleasant evening. Good-night." And he walked out, obsequiously preceded by Steiner.

St. Arnaud and Gavin were left alone. They had, however, seen a soldier standing in the corridor upon which the room opened, and outside they heard the steady tramp of the sentry's feet upon the frozen snow, as he marched up and down. The candles were burnt to their sockets, and the darkness was only illumined by the red glow of the stove. In silence they wrapped themselves in their pelisses, and lay down, not to sleep, but to discuss in whispers their chances.

"Why did you not accept your parole?" whispered Gavin.

"Because I believed our chances better as prisoners of war, and, besides, there was a question as to your parole. All this may be known some day," replied St. Arnaud in the same low whisper. "And you forget—Madame Ziska. No doubt we will be carried to Glatz, and she will be taken with us that far. I do not fear a very strict imprisonment—and a woman can contrive wonderful things."

" Some women can, like my mother, for example," replied Gavin.

" Very well. Madame Ziska is a loyal and devoted woman—something assures me of that; and, after all, we are not more than three hundred miles from Prince Charles at this very moment. Go to sleep."

Gavin remained quiet for five minutes. Then he whispered:

" Have you any money ? "

" Only a little, but half of it is yours."

Gavin nudged St. Arnaud with his elbow as a sign of gratitude, and was again quiet for five minutes, when he murmured: " We are much better off, even as prisoners, than we were last night."

" Yes."

" And," again whispered Gavin ʾdiffidently, " how did I act the officer ? "

" Admirably. All you needed was a sword."

" I can capture one from the enemy in time. Do you think His Majesty will be as pleasant to us in the morning ? "

" Not if he is like the kings I have known. The

more friendly and companionable the night before, the more surly the next morning—to keep us from presuming, I suppose."

A silence followed, and the deep and heavy breathing, which showed they had laid aside all their perplexities for that night.

About half an hour afterward, so Gavin imagined, he was awakened by St. Arnaud stirring about the room, but it was nearly daybreak. Like a true soldier, Gavin waked with all his wits about him. He saw St. Arnaud, after lighting a candle, produce a kettle from the closet in which they had been shut up, and, filling it with water, he put it on the stove, which was still glowing hot. As soon as the water boiled St. Arnaud, again going to the closet, fished out a basin, and proceeded to enjoy a thorough bath. He then produced his silver-mounted razor and, standing before a mirror, removed the beard which had appeared upon his face during the last twenty-four hours. Then, completely washed and shaved, he looked ready for a promenade in Paris. Gavin watched him closely, thinking to himself:

" He will see that I bathe and shave as carefully as he."

St. Arnaud's toilet finished, he shook Gavin, who

got up and made rather ostentatiously a toilet, if anything, more careful than St. Arnaud's. When it was over the two men were perfect pictures of officer-like neatness. And as for good looks, St. Arnaud was exquisitely handsome, while Gavin, by his noble figure, his brilliant complexion, and his frank and winning expression, made up for his want of regular beauty.

The tread of the sentry outside of the window was still heard, and men were passing back and forth in the corridors, and up and down the stairs. Scarcely was the gray dawn visible when their door was unceremoniously opened, and a trooper appeared, and, pointing with his sword toward the hall, St. Arnaud and Gavin went out. Awaiting them they found some bread and coffee for breakfast, and the Prussians fared no better.

On what had once been a well-kept pleasure ground, with a fish-pond in the middle, the King's staff and escort were assembled—over two hundred mounted men. A trooper held the bridles of the prisoners' horses, and Madame Ziska's comfortable travelling calash was drawn up in the centre of the cavalcade.

In another moment Madame Ziska appeared, a Prussian officer leading her down the steps.

She nodded to St. Arnaud and Gavin, saying gayly:

"I know not where we are going; but, being captives to His Majesty, we will neither starve nor freeze, of which there was great danger yesterday."

Down the steps presently came Frederick. He wore the shabby surtout of the night before, and his hat was a captain's cocked hat, with a tarnished silver buckle. His face was pale and his eyes heavy, as if he had spent the night awake. Behind him walked poor Steiner, carrying a large bundle of dispatches, and almost yawning in the King's face from sleeplessness. Immediately the King's horse was brought, and he mounted. His staff assembled around him, and the order was given to start. All this time he had not bestowed a word or a look upon Madame Ziska in her calash or the two prisoners. On passing them, however, he recognized their salutes by an absent-minded bow. Gavin, who was totally unprepared for this change, muttered to St. Arnaud:

"Nice behaviour, that; I suppose His Majesty has quite forgotten that he pulled me out of the closet last night, and he laughed like a schoolboy at it!"

"Put not your trust in princes," was St. Arnaud's whispered reply.

They then put forward rapidly and in silence. The morning was clear and cold, and they travelled fast. Shortly after sunrise they reached a place where the highroad branched in two. A halt was made, and Frederick, who had been riding ahead, stopped, and a part of the escort defiled before him. When Madame Ziska's calash approached, behind which rode St. Arnaud and Gavin, Frederick rode up to them. His eyes were sparkling, his figure was erect, and the agreeable voice for which he was celebrated rang out musically.

"We part here, madame and messieurs," he said. "Gentlemen, you are for Glatz. Madame for anywhere she likes. I to meet Prince Charles of Lorraine wherever I can find him. I have to thank you for a pleasant evening. *Bon jour!*" And putting spurs to his horse, and followed by a dozen officers, he was gone.

"What strange creatures are kings!" was Gavin's comment to St. Arnaud, who, in his time, had seen much of royalty. "Glatz! A terrible place to be imprisoned in!"

"There is a way out of every place to which there is a way in," was St. Arnaud's reply.

That night they stopped at a village where Prussians were much in evidence; and three days afterward, at nightfall, they found themselves at the main entrance of the fortress of Glatz.

Madame Ziska was still with them, but her behaviour during their three days of journeying had surprised and disgusted Gavin. She seemed rather to avoid them, and was hand and glove with the Prussians. Gavin had mentioned it several times to St. Arnaud, who only smiled and said: " Women go by contraries sometimes, my lad."

When the moment came, before the gate of the citadel of Glatz, that the two were to part from her, she stepped from her carriage lightly, and said good-by with a gayety which seemed to Gavin quite heartless. It was a bright moonlight evening, and the lights in the town shone cheerfully. But before them loomed the fortress, black and forbidding. For the first time Gavin's heart sank; it sank lower still when this woman, whom he had credited with the utmost generosity of heart, showed such indifference to their fate.

" I will remain here a day or two," she said, " until I can get post-horses. I wish I could do something for you; perhaps I may be able to send you some delicacies for your table. We may hope to meet again; I, an actress, singer, and dancer, go up and down the world earning my living, and I meet everybody in the world at least once, and sometimes twice. I shall not soon forget that evening we spent as the King's prisoners. Remember me. Adieu."

The two prisoners were taken before the commandant of the fortress, General Kollnitz, who received them courteously as prisoners of war, and invited them to supper with him. He was of unwieldy bulk, but clear-eyed and clear-headed, and, evidently, a capable man. The only other guest at the table was the adjutant, Pfels, whom St. Arnaud and Gavin found an amiable and soldierly young man.

Gavin by that time had grown so used to sitting at the table with officers, that he felt not only as if he really were an officer, but as if he had always been an officer. He could not rally, however, from his depression. The falsity, as he thought, of Madame Ziska affected him strangely. Naturally, he took his mother as the standard of all women, and he looked for high courage and unswerving loyalty from them all. True, they had no claim on Madame Ziska, but he thought her a brave and honest woman, and St. Arnaud had hinted at chances of

assistance from her which had impressed the idea
upon him that they might look to her for succour.
So he ate his supper silently, while St. Arnaud
spared no pains in making himself agreeable to
the commandant. He told the story of their capture
inimitably, and had the fat general and the slim ·
adjutant both laughing at it, especially at Gavin's
assertion that if only he had kept his wits about
him he would have knocked the King down.

At last, supper being over, they were shown two
communicating cells high up in the tower of the
fortress. A candle was given them, the door
locked, and they were left alone. St. Arnaud at
once blew out the candle, hid it, and the two, sitting on Gavin's bed, with the moonlight streaming
through a narrow, barred window, realized that
they were prisoners. And in the very first hour
of their real captivity they began to plan for
their escape. Gavin's first words were: "You
counted on Madame Ziska; what think you
now?"

"I think," responded St. Arnaud, with a smile,
"that an honest woman like her is more to be
trusted than the great ones of earth. Look at our
friend the King—singing and drinking with us at
night, parting from us in the morning, without

asking us if we were in want, or if he could do the smallest thing for us."

" Humph! Madame Ziska offered to send us something to eat if she had time and could remember it. And she hardly spoke to us after we started on the journey."

" Did you expect her to set all eyes to watching us by promising us eternal friendship? Now hear me: Madame Ziska's manner convinced me that she meant to help us substantially; and her coldness to us was intended to throw the rest off the scent. I can tell you this much: I shall very carefully examine any provender that Madame Ziska may chance to remember to send us. I knew a woman once who sent a jewel in an orange. They are, after all, much cleverer than we. Think about that until you go to sleep."

CHAPTER IV

THE first week of captivity passed slowly and heavily for Gavin and St. Arnaud, and it was not lightened when, a few days after, came the news of the defeat of Prince Charles at Leuthen by Frederick of Prussia.

Naturally, every waking hour was spent in planning and dreaming of escape, but St. Arnaud counselled patience.

"Wait until we know something more of our surroundings and the people about us. I have an idea in my mind about the commandant. And, besides, we shall hear from Madame Ziska in time, and I have the greatest confidence in that woman's friendship." To all of which Gavin gave a grumbling assent.

In that time, St. Arnaud and Gavin, who, a month before, had never exchanged a word, came to know each other better than they knew any other men in the world. Gavin's trustful and generous nature was filled with admiration at the calmness

61

and even gayety with which St. Arnaud bore his misfortunes. He made a careful toilet every day, sang and whistled cheerfully, and amused himself and Gavin, too, by supplying what he called the deficiencies of a limited education. He studied German industriously, and succeeded in borrowing from the commandant a few old books on military science, which he read with diligence if not with profit.

" You see," he said to Gavin, " I was taught no end of Latin and Greek and music and grammar and fencing, and all sorts of things that an officer should know; but this original person, the King of Prussia, has made all these things perfectly useless. Some of our generals whom he has defeated knew more Latin and Greek and fencing than I; but yet they were whipped. However, if England, your country, will continue to assist the Empress Queen, we may yet beat Frederick. And meanwhile I am doing my best to study the art of war, although, according to the books, the King's tactics are all wrong."

Gavin would smile at this and listen, but left to himself, he had not the calm fortitude of the older man. Nothing in the way of danger or privation could quench Gavin's spirit as long as he

was on horseback and roaming about the country;
but the confinement of a prison for a week did more
to depress him than a month of dangers and haz-
ards. Often he would toss about on his narrow
bed and groan loudly in the very anguish of his
heart, and then be shamed into fortitude by St.
Arnaud laughing at him. And St. Arnaud declined to consider either of them the most unfortunate of men.

"I grant you," said he, "that I would rather
be at Versailles, as I was a year ago, than shut up
here in Glatz. But the other was an imprisonment, too. What do you think of getting up at
five o'clock, spending the whole day in attendance
on the King, in court clothes and periwig? Ah!
how hot it was in summer, and how cold it was
in winter! Never a moment to sit down, always
wearing a grin, when one would much rather have
scowled. I was freer when I was a captain in Dufour's regiment than ever I was in the King's
Musketeers, where even the private soldiers are
gentlemen."

"But we will *never* get out. Prince Charles
beaten, what is there to keep that long-nosed Frederick from marching to Vienna? Tell me that, I
say."

"Don't trouble yourself about that. Let us see how we can get to Vienna ourselves. It is time we were hearing from Madame Ziska, for I am sure she has not forgotten us."

The very next morning a parcel was brought them, with an unsealed letter. All had been opened and the letter read. It ran:

"DEAR CAPTAIN ST. ARNAUD: Knowing you and your fellow-prisoner, Sublieutenant Hamilton, were well fed by the excellent commandant, I had difficulty in thinking of something you needed. But remembering how excessively particular you are about your toilet, I send you some powder and scented soap. I am leaving here to-day in hopes of some time reaching Vienna, where I expect to find an engagement at the opera house. I shall stop a few days on the road with some relatives of mine, honest shopkeepers. How strange is life! One day I sup with the greatest king in the world; the next I visit people who hang a bag of wool in one window and a hank of yarn in the other, to signify what they have to sell. I scorn, as you see, the common affectation of representing my family to be more important than it really is.

"I beg you both to hold me in remembrance, and I promise not to forget you. We shall meet again.   ROSA ZISKA."

The soap bore evident marks of having been pricked through with darning-needles, to make sure that neither files nor money were concealed inside. Nevertheless, as soon as they were locked up for the night Gavin and St. Arnaud proceeded to dissolve the soap in a basin of water by the light of the brilliant moon, which flooded their cells through the narrow window. They were rewarded by finding small scraps of paper, so cunningly laid inside the soap that a needle could pass through it without trouble. After carefully saving every scrap and drying them all, daylight revealed them to be, when pieced together, a bank-note for a hundred ducats and a map of the country around Glatz, showing, in particular, the road to the Bohemian mountains. Several villages on the route were marked by crosses, indicating it was safe to stop at them.

"And I thought she had forgotten us!" said Gavin remorsefully.

"Women, my dear boy, rarely desert us in misfortune. They carefully choose our time of prosperity to play the deuce. They are considerate even in tormenting us. One thing is sure about this particular woman, Madame Ziska—she thinks us a couple of enterprising fellows, and evidently expects us to escape, and I cannot bear to disappoint the expectations of a lady."

"It seems to me," said Gavin, "that for prisoners captured by the King's own hand we have very little attention shown us by the commandant. He might have asked us to dinner, at least."

The very next morning Pfels, the tall, thin adjutant, appeared with the compliments of General Kollnitz and an invitation to dinner at four o'clock. Pfels, who was a very civil, pleasant fellow, explained that this would have been done before, but that the commandant had been suffering from rheumatism, and had been obliged to keep his bed for some time past. His health, however, was now restored.

The invitation was promptly accepted, and then Gavin began to tease St. Arnaud to tell him the plan of escape in which the commandant figured. St. Arnaud good-naturedly refused, and then Gavin cried:

"But let us swear never to be divided from each

other, for I believe our chance of safety is increased
tenfold by being together."

St. Arnaud smiled; he read Gavin like a book,
and saw that this pretence of finding safety together was only the heart of Gavin clinging to what
it loved.

Precisely at a quarter to four Pfels appeared,
and led them through a maze of corridors, stairs,
and passages, to the commandant's quarters.
These were a handsome suite of rooms, directly
on the sallyport.

On entering, they found General Kollnitz seated
in a huge chair; he managed to rise from it, in
spite of his vast bulk and stiff joints, to welcome
his guests.

" You will find us a small party," said he, " but
the fact is we are very short of officers at present,
the King having need of all that could be spared,
and my military family is much reduced."

Dinner was soon announced, and proved an excellent one. St. Arnaud exerted himself, as usual,
to be agreeable, and he never failed at that. Gavin,
too, recovered his spirits at the sight of a good dinner, and sent the fat general into roars of laughter
by saying, when Frederick's name was mentioned:

" And to think I should have been led, like a

great calf, out of that closet! Oh, I am afraid the King thinks me a wretched coward!"

The dinner passed pleasantly, and Gavin's heart was made glad by a polite offer from General Koll- nitz to forward letters for them. Gavin immedi- ately began in thought a letter to his mother.

Evidences of vigilance and watchfulness on the part of the garrison were not wanting, even when the commandant and his adjutant were supposed to be taking their ease at dinner. Every hour Pfels was called into the anteroom to receive reports from every quarter of the fortress. About half-past eight o'clock the general, who had been talking gayly, suddenly stopped, laid his head back, and in a moment was slumbering peacefully. Pfels smiled and said: "That has been his habit for years. He is quite unconscious of it, though, and if you hint he has been asleep he grows very angry. He wakes of himself in a half hour or so, and goes back to what he was talking about when he dropped off. I was warned, when I was ordered here, that more aides had been sent back to their regiments for mentioning to the general that he had fallen asleep than one could count. It is quite the garri- son joke."

Sure enough, as Pfels said, the general waked

after a while and resumed: " Gentlemen, as we
were saying a moment ago, your letters should be
ready to-morrow." None of the young men as
much as smiled.

At nine o'clock the rumbling of a carriage under
the archway was heard.

" That is no new arrival," remarked General
Kollnitz. " The regulations require me to make
the circuit of the fortress, inside and out, at nine
o'clock every evening. My disabilities compel me
to make the outer circuit in a carriage. But, let
none think that the only inspection had is that of a
gouty old gentleman, the rattling of whose carriage may be heard a mile off. That is merely
perfunctory. Better legs and eyes than mine are
on watch day and night. Not a prisoner has escaped since I have been here, and every deserter
has been recaptured. On all three sides of the
fortress a heavy siege-gun is kept loaded, and as
soon as a prisoner or deserter is missed, those guns
are fired, one immediately after the other. That
gives notice, and arouses not only the garrison,
but the town and the surrounding country. As I
offer a handsome reward for every prisoner or
deserter captured, the peasants and townspeople
may be relied on for vigilance; and difficult as the

escape is from the fortress, the real obstruction is outside and beyond the walls. I tell you this for your profit, because, being young and adventurous, you may tempt fate; and you will certainly fail unless you can get at least two hours' start before your absence is discovered."

Pfels then went to a press in the room, and took out a huge cloak and chapeau, which he placed upon the general; and, putting on his own cloak and hat, and calling an orderly to show the guests the way back to their cells, opened the door and carefully escorted the rheumatic old gentleman down a winding stair. Gavin and St. Arnaud heard the clank of muskets as the guard presented arms, and in another moment the carriage rolled under the sallyport.

The next day Gavin spent writing to his mother. He covered many pages, and when Pfels made his rounds that evening handed him the letter. It was well written and well expressed, and Gavin felt decidedly proud of his educational accomplishments. Pfels made a polite apology for being compelled to read the letter before sending it.

" Read it now," cried Gavin.

Pfels glanced over it, and handed it back with a smile.

"Pardon me for calling your attention to a singular circumstance; you have not told your mother one word about yourself, as far as I have seen; it is all about your fellow-prisoner."

"Oh!" cried Gavin with a blush. "Give me the letter;" and he added at the bottom: "Dear mother, forgive me for forgetting to tell you that I am very well. Your devoted son, G. H."

So agreeable was the impression made by the two upon the commandant, that they were invited to dine with him constantly. Life in the fortress was monotonous to the officers, and the presence of two interesting prisoners was a genuine resource to the commandant and Pfels. St. Arnaud and Gavin had by no means given up the thought of escape, in spite of the general's well-meant warning; and as the prospect of exchange grew fainter, they dwelt the more upon the idea of getting away. Both of them realized the numerous difficulties they would encounter, even if they should be fortunate enough to get beyond the walls; yet that did not cause them to give up their hopes. One night, after they had been dining with the commandant and Pfels, and were returned to their cells, St. Arnaud whispered:

"Do you know. Gavin, I think you look some-

71

thing like the general. Of course, you are not so large, but a couple of pillows, and the general's cloak and hat—"

"What!" replied Gavin, in an indignant whisper; for this young man had no small opinion of his own comeliness of face and figure; and then suddenly stopping, he realized a hidden meaning in St. Arnaud's words. The two conversed half the night in whispers; and when, toward morning, they dropped off asleep, St. Arnaud was saying: "All's fair in war, as in love."

They anxiously awaited another invitation to dine, and when the invitation and the day came they were ready for something more than a dinner with the general and Pfels. St. Arnaud had given Gavin half the money he had left; poor Gavin had only a few francs of his private's pay remaining. Gavin carried the bank-note concealed about him, and St. Arnaud the map. Each had in his pocket his comb and soap and such poor preparations as could be made for flight; and each, on leaving the cell, gave a last look back, and knew that he would never enter it again, for before nine o'clock they meant to make a dash for liberty, and if they failed and were brought back, they would be consigned to a far more rigorous confinement.

General Kollnitz received them with his usual
kindness, and Gavin felt a qualm at the thought
of the perplexity and chagrin in which they were
about to plunge the old gentleman. Liberty, however, was too dear to be forsworn; and they both
knew it to be their duty, as well as their right, to
make every effort to restore their services to their
own country. Thoughts of the same kind had
passed through St. Arnaud's brain, and he had said
to Gavin the night before:

"Our oath obliges us to do all in our power to
annoy the enemy. Egad, we will annoy the enemy
fearfully in this case—poor, dear old Kollnitz! I
believe he will be more annoyed at having his
record broken than at the loss of our valuable
company; that is, if—" St. Arnaud made a significant pause.

Neither he nor Gavin indicated by the flutter
of an eyelash that a moment of destiny was approaching. The short January twilight made
candles necessary before dinner was half over,
and then a heavy fog crept down the mountains,
and enveloped town and fortress in a white
and death-like mist. The ground was covered
with snow, and General Kollnitz shivered as he
said:

"Ugh! To take my rheumatism out a night like this!"

By what seemed a strange fatality the conversation turned on escapes from prison, and the general said frankly: "I pride myself not on the strength of my bolts and bars, but on the inability of an escaped prisoner or deserter to get beyond the radius in which he is sure to be captured. I believe it has been proved that human ingenuity can break through any bond which human ingenuity can devise. But under my system every peasant within ten miles is made a scout the instant the guns are fired; and the prospect of a hundred florins sharpens their wits amazingly."

Gavin and St. Arnaud frankly agreed with him that the real difficulties existed outside rather than inside the prison.

Dinner over, the servants left the room, and pipes were produced; but St. Arnaud and Gavin had not acquired the practice of smoking, common even then among Prussian officers. General Kollnitz was a picture as he sat back, his huge form filling his chair, with a long pipe in front of him. Pfels was no less active and vigilant than ever; at six, seven, and eight o'clock he went into the anteroom to receive the report of the officer of the guard, and at nine he was to make the tour of the fortress with the commandant.

By eight o'clock the commandant was taking his usual doze. Pfels went out into the anteroom, and as soon as his back was turned Gavin rose and, taking a knife from the table, softly cut all the cords from the curtains and bell-ropes, and quickly rolled them into a pile, which he threw on the sofa, and carefully placed the sofa-cushions over them. Then he gently tried the handle of the closet door in which the general's huge pelisse and hat and Pfels' hat and cloak were kept, and, to his joy, all were hanging in their accustomed places. When Pfels returned he found St. Arnaud and Gavin still seated at the table, and apparently absorbed in a game of patience, while the commandant snored loudly.

" The commandant's practice of going to sleep over his pipe is rather awkward with certain guests," said Pfels, laughing and reseating himself at the table, " but nothing can change his habit. Luckily, I keep wide-awake enough for two."

" We don't object in the least to the commandant's taking his ease, although we enjoy his company; but I observe, unlike most inert men, he keeps other people's eyes open."

The three young men continued to converse pleasantly until the hand of the clock pointed to ten minutes before nine. Then Gavin rose and, going to the window which was at Pfels' back, peered out. The solid mass of the fortress, the town, the river, the snow-covered earth, all were wrapped in a white veil of fog, through which they loomed mysteriously. This cold and silvery mist brought with it silence as well as obscurity. All sounds were deadened, and the dim figures of the sentries, as they passed to and fro, were like ghosts, so noiseless were their steps. The thought came into Gavin's mind, "The guns will not carry far to-night." At that moment there was the slight commotion outside of relieving the guard, and Pfels said to St. Arnaud:

"My work for the day will soon be over. Bohm is officer in charge to-night, and I always feel particularly safe when he—"

The next instant Gavin pinioned him from behind, and St. Arnaud slipped a gag made of the playing-cards and a napkin into the poor adjutant's mouth. He had not a moment to cry out, and could not utter an articulate sound; and the slight scuffle he was able to make, while his hands and feet were securely tied with bell cords by St. Ar-

76

naud, could not be heard outside the room. He was then blindfolded with a napkin, St. Arnaud saying:

"Sorry, dear Pfels, but, you know, it is a soldier's duty to escape if he can, and you would do as much by me. You are one of the best fellows in the world "—here he fixed the gag more firmly in the mouth of poor Pfels, who groaned faintly— "and as you and the general often told us getting out of the fortress was nothing—we were certain to be caught within two hours—so, now, we will have a chance to test our respective theories."

Pfels could only writhe about and wag his head violently; but they thought it as well to tie him to his chair, a precaution which they also took with the general, as he slumbered peacefully.

All was done in an almost inconceivably short time. They dared not turn the lock of the door for fear of awaking suspicion in the anteroom, but as no one would enter without knocking, they could safely count on a few minutes of time. St. Arnaud noiselessly opened the door of the press and got out the general's best cloak and chapeau, while Gavin firmly tied a couple of sofa-pillows around his body; and when he had on the huge cloak, with the collar turned up to his eyes, and the chapeau

77

pulled down over his ears, it was not a bad imitation of the general's grotesque figure. St. Arnaud put on Pfels' cloak and hat, and they looked at the clock and saw that they had yet five minutes to wait.

St. Arnaud went to the door of the anteroom, and kept his hand on the key, ready to turn it at a moment's notice, while Gavin carried out the last detail of their carefully studied plan by stuffing bits of his handkerchief in the ears of Pfels and the commandant. They had then four minutes to wait for the carriage, and it was the longest interval of time that either one was ever to spend in his life.

The roll of the carriage was then heard, and in another moment they had softly opened the door that led to the stairs, and were going lightly down.

They came down so much quicker than the commandant usually did, that the orderly, who was standing on the pavement a little way off, did not have time to open the carriage door; St. Arnaud, however, saved him the trouble, and, as he ran forward, Pfels, as he thought, was just stepping into the carriage. The orderly put up the steps, jumped on the box, and the coachman drove through the sallyport, the orderly giving the countersign.

CHAPTER V

THEY were soon across the drawbridge and outside the ramparts. The night was pitch dark, but
in spite of it the coachman drove rapidly along the
well-known road, and they were not stopped once
after getting outside. As soon as they were on
the side of the citadel opposite the town, they knew
they were on the side of the Bohemian mountains.
This was their point of escape. Gavin disengaged
himself of his pillows and threw the heavy cloak
over his arm, and St. Arnaud did likewise; they
could not afford to cast away such excellent dis-
guises. Then, noiselessly opening the carriage
door, they both dropped to the ground with so
much dexterity that they managed to shut the door,
so its banging might not attract the orderly's attention. They thus found themselves outside the
fortress within fifteen minutes of the time they
had escaped. They stopped and listened for
a moment, but evidently no alarm had yet been
given.

"We shall hear the guns, though, as soon as the carriage reaches the postern gate, if not before; and after that—" said St. Arnaud.

Gavin only pointed before them. "Yonder are the mountains. We cannot see them—so much the better—no one can see us. The frontier is twenty English miles away, and we should gain it before daylight."

With the blood leaping in their veins at the thought of liberty, even for an hour, they plunged forward through the fog. The snow made walking difficult, but they felt as light of foot as the chamois among the hills. They sped along in spite of every obstacle, and when, within half an hour, the report of the three alarm guns rumbled through the heavy air, they had already gained a considerable distance. The darkness and the fog made it impossible for them to know precisely in what direction they were going; they only knew that they had got among fields and hedgerows, which they ardently hoped were in the direction of the mountains. Gavin, however, in the long marches of the past campaign had got something of the soldier's instinct for the right road, and when toward midnight the fog lifted and a pallid moon came forth, they found they were on the right track for the mountains, although they had not come as straight as they had hoped.

At intervals they had heard faint and distant sounds indicating pursuit; but the damp air stifled sound. At midnight, though, when it suddenly cleared, they heard afar off the tramping of hoofs. They found themselves on a by-road, where there were hedges, but no trees, and farmhouses were scattered about. All was as still as death except for that light but ominous echo of advancing horses and men. The sound was coming nearer, and the hoof-beats could be distinctly heard.

In front of them was a farmstead, with good outbuildings, including a cattle shed and stables. The snow was much trodden thereabouts, so that their tracks would not betray them. They found both the shed and the stable doors locked, but the stable window was left open for ventilation. They crawled in the window, and found a ladder leading to the loft, which was stored with hay. In two minutes they were concealed under it. In ten minutes more a squad of cavalry had ridden up, and every farmhouse was astir with the news they brought. Two prisoners had escaped, and the commandant would pay a hundred florins for either of them. The stable door was flung open, and the

farmer who owned the place and his two sons saddled the horses, arranging their plans in full hearing of the fugitives just above their heads. The
business of the squad of cavalry was to arouse the
country, rather than personally hunt for the fugitives. They soon passed on, therefore, and in a
little while most of the men in the hamlet had
joined in the search, while the rest returned to bed.

The hay in the loft was warm and dry, and Gavin and St. Arnaud were terribly fatigued, and
they longed to take rest until morning; but the
hours of darkness were precious to them. They
waited until everything had quieted down, and then,
starting forth from their hiding-place, resumed the
march toward the mountains.

They trudged along, somewhat guided by their
map, and although they caught sight more than
once of pursuing parties, they managed to conceal
themselves, but they knew they could not expect to
be so fortunate in broad daylight.

The dawn came clear and beautiful, and bearing
no trace of the fog of the night before. The Bohemian mountains, only ten English miles away, loomed
darkly beautiful on the horizon. The snow lay
deep upon the whole earth when the first golden
shafts of light struck the mountain-tops from the

east; as the sun rose in glory, they glowed milk
white against a sky all blue and gold and rose-
coloured. Gavin and St. Arnaud saw the exquisite
sunrise with heavy hearts; a clear day made the
chances of their eluding pursuit for ten miles still
more hazardous. They were half dead with fatigue, after their weeks of close confinement; they
were foot-sore and hungry, but their spirits were
unfaltering, and no word of complaint escaped
them.

They had avoided the highway, although they
knew that every lane, by-road, and hedgerow would
be searched for them; and as the day fully broke,
they found themselves in a pleasant rolling country,
somewhat off the usual line of travel, with many
houses of a good class, but barren of woods. Immediately before them was a pleasant villa, with a
tall yew hedge all around it. As they trudged past
they noticed a kind of natural alcove in the hedge,
in which they were tolerably concealed from view;
and they threw themselves down for a moment
to rest their weary limbs and study their rude
map.

Soon they heard merry voices and laughter on
the other side of the hedge. Two milkmaids were
at their work, and as the milk foamed into the

pails they laughed and chatted about the events of the night before.

" Such a night! " cried one. " Troopers all over the place at one o'clock in the morning; and Miss Hein screamed so loud when the officer caught her in her curl papers that he thought she had certainly concealed the two prisoners in the house."

"How sorry I am to have missed it! " replied the other one. " This place is so dull, nothing happening from one week's end to another, that I even like the notion of being routed out as you were last night. The truth is, I don't fancy living with these quiet, prim ladies, like Miss Hein. I would rather live in a large family, with plenty of servants, and gay doings below stairs."

Gavin peeped through an opening in the hedge. The milkmaid plunged into a description of the adventures of the night before, when the house and offices had been searched for the two fugitives; and in the excitement of her tale she stopped milking. Her back and that of her companion was toward Gavin, and the milk bucket was just within reach of his arm. He noiselessly thrust his arm through the opening and, reaching the milk pail, raised it as high as he could, and St. Arnaud, tiptoeing over the hedge, took it. There was about a

quart of milk in it, and first St. Arnaud taking a
pull at it, and then Gavin, it was emptied in a
minute. Gavin's long arm then replaced it, and
they resumed their places of concealment. A
shriek of dismay presently informed them that the
milkmaid had found her bucket empty. The cow
having strayed off, too, there was great excitement
for a while, but both the women moved away from
the hedge, marvelling the while over the strange
disappearance of the milk.

St. Arnaud, turning to Gavin, said: "We shall
be caught before twelve o'clock if we attempt to
make across the country in this clear weather.
This place has been searched once, and is not likely
to be searched again. I believe our best chance is
to remain here."

" How ? " asked Gavin.

" I will show you, if you will have confidence in
me."

A look was Gavin's only answer to this.

St. Arnaud then, with Gavin, made his way boldly to the front door of the house and knocked loudly.
Another maid opened the door, and from the smirk
she wore, she, too, thought it rather amusing to
have a sensation occasionally as they had had the
night before. But there was no smirk upon the

face of Miss Hein, a tall, thin, lugubrious-looking lady, with a not unkind face, who appeared behind her.

"Madam," said St. Arnaud to Miss Hein, with a low bow, "I hear that you were very much disturbed last night by the searching of your house for two runaways from the fortress. I have come to make you every apology. We are officers, as you see. The officer last night was a mere subaltern, and, although zealous, he evidently did not know how to perform an unpleasant duty."

"He certainly did not," replied Miss Hein tartly.

"Ah, madam," cried St. Arnaud sentimentally, "would that I had come in the first instance! I would not have disturbed you in the least. Any complaint you have to make about the officer or men I will attend to with pleasure."

Miss Hein, whose placid house had been the scene of such unusual turmoil, was immensely pleased at the different tone that this supposed Prussian officer took with her, and bowing politely, invited them to enter. "And as you have probably been all night searching for the fugitives, you must be both tired and hungry, and I will have breakfast for you."

Gavin could hardly restrain a shout of joy.

Miss Hein took them into a comfortable sitting-room on the first floor, and while waiting for breakfast to be prepared St. Arnaud made such good use of his time and tongue that the poor lady was completely won over. He begged that she would give them the honour of her presence while they breakfasted, which she graciously did. St. Arnaud asked if handbills had yet reached them describing the escaped prisoners, and with a deep feeling of joy heard they had not. At this Gavin said for the benefit of the servant waiting on them, as well as Miss Hein:

" I can tell you what they are like. St. Arnaud is a great big, red-headed fellow with a terrible squint—you would know the man to be a rascal anywhere. His manners are harsh, and his voice is like sawing wood with a dull saw."

St. Arnaud, determined not to be outdone, broke in : " And the other one, Hamilton by name, would be taken for a girl dressed up in man's clothes—a weak, puling creature, and universally considered the ugliest man in the French army."

" Do you hear that, Martha ? " said Miss Hein to the maid. " Remember it and tell the other servants."

A good breakfast had very much raised the spirits of the two fugitives, but they realized that they were in jeopardy every moment. St. Arnaud, after reflecting a moment, said to Miss Hein: "Would it be asking too much of your kindness to let a couple of tired Prussian officers sleep a few hours in your house? We have been travelling all night—I will explain later why we have no horses—and we are overcome with fatigue."

"Certainly," replied Miss Hein, who had been completely won by her amiable guests. "I myself am leaving in my travelling chaise this afternoon, to pay a visit of some days in the town of Glatz, and I will take you both with pleasure. The chaise seats four. Meanwhile, you may take your rest in an upper chamber. I am glad to show hospitality to officers who know so well how to treat a helpless woman."

They were shown upstairs into a comfortable room with two beds. As they shut and locked the door, they looked earnestly at each other. St. Arnaud, without a word, tumbled into one of the beds, saying: "We may never come out of this room alive; but let us take our rest calmly. We are in the hands of fate."

"In the hands of God, you mean—so my mother

taught me," answered Gavin; and straightway he
plumped down on his knees at the side of the bed,
and said a prayer out aloud for their success in
escaping; and then, throwing himself on the bed,
was asleep in two minutes.

St. Arnaud waked first. There was a clock in
the room, and he saw that it was five o'clock, and
the short winter twilight was coming on. He shook
Gavin, and in a few moments they went downstairs. Miss Hein, in her riding-dress, was walking up and down the hall impatiently. "I am
afraid," she said, "it is too late to make our
start."

"That is unfortunate," responded St. Arnaud.
"Would you, however, permit us to use your chaise
to the next posting-house, which cannot be more
than two miles away?"

Miss Hein cogitated for a moment. But there
was a sweet persuasiveness in St. Arnaud's tone
that she had not been able to resist since the first
hour she met him, and she answered pleasantly:

"Yes. You have been so polite—"

"Oh, madam, it is you—it is your kindness—
and trust me, it will never be forgotten."

The chaise was before the door, and Gavin and
St. Arnaud, bidding an adieu so warm that it

brought the blood to Miss Hein's faded cheek, went out and entered the carriage. The coachman, a country lout, drove off in the direction of Glatz. As soon as they were out of sight of the house, St. Arnaud put his head out of the window and said:

"You are going in the wrong direction. It is the next posting-house toward the mountains that we wish to reach." The rustic turned his horses about, and they travelled toward the mountains for four miles. They were too intent upon listening for pursuit and surprise to speak much, but Gavin said: " It is not often that escaped prisoners ride in coaches and chaises, as we have done."

"Good Miss Hein!" cried St. Arnaud. " I had half a mind to throw ourselves on her mercy. I believe there is scarcely a woman who lives who will not be kind to an unfortunate."

At the next posting-house they had no trouble in securing horses, Miss Hein's chaise and servants being well known. The postmaster and all the people were asking about the fugitives, and several detachments of soldiers had visited the place that day. St. Arnaud, talking with the postmaster, carelessly asked if descriptive handbills had been posted yet.

"We are expecting them every moment," replied the man.

St. Arnaud then gave a personal description which could not possibly apply to either himself or Gavin; and, asking for a private room, wrote Miss Hein a note full of gratitude, to which he signed a German name. The chaise they had ordered soon appeared, and in a little while they were travelling toward the frontier.

When night fell they were entering a little mountain village marked with a cross on their map; and, driving through the steep and straggling street, they came to a shop with a bag of wool hanging in one window and a hank of yarn in the other.

They knocked, and were asked to enter by a pleasant-faced woman. The house was a kind of a rude inn, as well as shop and dwelling, and half a dozen peasants were gathered around a fire on which a pot was boiling. St. Arnaud spoke two words—"Madame Ziska"—in the woman's ear, and she responded by an intelligent look.

"This is no place for your honours," she said; "I have a little room off that I can give you."

She led them into a small room, scarcely more

than a shed, and shut the door. "I have change for a hundred ducats," she whispered. "My cousin—for so Madame Ziska is, although I am not fit to be her waiting-maid—told me to give you that much money out of my savings, and you would give me a bank-note for it."

They quickly made the exchange, and both eagerly asked for news of Madame Ziska, but there was none since she had passed through the village on her way to Vienna.

Supper was presently served—the first meal St. Arnaud and Gavin had eaten in liberty since the first night of their meeting. They were waited on by a tall, handsome, intelligent-looking girl, Bettina, the niece of the hostess. She took them for Prussian officers, and showed them the utmost ill-will. She nearly knocked Gavin's head off with a platter when he turned to ask her some simple question, and scowled blackly at St. Arnaud when he airily threw her a kiss. They were in uproariously high spirits, although they kept their voices down as much as possible.

"This is magnificent," cried St. Arnaud, ladling cabbage soup into his mouth. "I have altogether lost my taste for paté de foie gras and champagne, in favor of cabbage soup and onions, bacon, and black bread. They are the real luxuries of life." To which Gavin agreed.

St. Arnaud then turned his attention to the sulky Bettina. " What a great stroke it would be if you capture those two fellows escaped from Glatz! You would get two hundred florins." No reply from Bettina, except a furious clattering of dishes. " You could get married with that portion," continued St. Arnaud.

" Not unless I meet some men who are a vast improvement on those who come here," retaliated Bettina, flouncing out angrily.

Presently the woman of the house entered and, after refusing to take any money for their entertainment, said: " You will find outside a cart and horse. They belong to me, so you may do as you like with them." She showed them a way out without passing through the front part of the house, and there, in the moonlight, was a rough country cart, and Bettina sitting in it to drive them. But what a change was in her! Eager, smiling, and obliging, she could do nothing at first but apologize for her rudeness. " I did not know you were Madame Ziska's friends," she protested a dozen times.

They mounted into the cart, and with thanks that came from the bottom of their hearts parted with their friend. They travelled on through the night, Bettina driving rapidly and skilfully. The moon sank, and then came the ghastly hour between night and day, and presently a sunrise more glorious than they had ever seen, for they were at liberty and in safety.

Bettina was to leave them at a small village across the frontier, where they hoped to get horses, but were far from certain. Hearing them discuss this, Bettina said: " If you like, you can buy this horse and cart. My aunt has been trying to sell them both for forty florins this month past; she wants to buy better ones."

" Here are fifty florins," joyfully cried St. Arnaud. " But how will you get back home ? "

" I can walk," nonchalantly replied Bettina, " and if I get tired on the way, I will wait for the carrier's cart, which goes to my village to-day."

She got down in the road, St. Arnaud handed her the money, and she made him promise to feed the horse well; and then St. Arnaud, proceeding, by way of reward, to give her a kiss, Bettina raised her strong arm and fetched him a thundering box on the ear; and Gavin, who was standing by quite innocent, inadvertently happening to laugh, Bettina gave him two corresponding slaps that nearly knocked him down, crying:

" Is that the way you behave ? I'll teach you better manners, both of you ! " and strode down the road indignantly, scorning to look back.

" I thought," said Gavin, rubbing his tingling cheeks, " that women were always kind to the unfortunate."

" Well, there are exceptions," diplomatically replied St. Arnaud. " For my own part, I am very much obliged to the young lady for not giving me a good beating; she is perfectly capable of it, physically as well as morally."

" And we are not unfortunates any longer," cried Gavin, jumping into the cart, and giving the patient horse a whack. " We are free, we have money, we have this equipage ! "

" Yes," replied St. Arnaud gayly, " we will not trouble with post-chaises; we will travel the whole distance to Vienna in this blessed cart; we will make our *entrée* as conspicuously as possible. We will drive under the palace windows of the Empress Queen herself, and let her see us. Oh, we will make such an arrival into Vienna that it won't be forgotten in a hurry ! "

" We will ! We will ! " shouted Gavin, belabouring, in the excess of his joy, the poor horse; " and we won't say anything about the fond adieu we had from Miss Bettina."

Some weeks after this, on a brilliant winter morning, the last day of the year, all Vienna was astir for a great military review. The Empress Queen, undaunted by the disasters at Rosbach and Leuthen, had determined to renew the contest with her old enemy, the King of Prussia, at the earliest practicable moment; and to give heart to her army and people, she appeared constantly before them, reviewed her troops often, and showed undiminished confidence in them. She had, it is true, consented that her brother-in-law, the Archduke Charles, should be relieved of the command of the army, in deference to the popular will. But she, the most loyal sovereign in the world to all who had served her, took occasion to soften the blow to the Archduke Charles by appearing with him in public and treating him with a kindness that his courage and devotion merited, although he had been vanquished by the superior genius of the King of Prussia. She had, therefore, ordered a grand review of the household troops, with a number of veterans of the last campaign. It was a means she took of keeping up the courage of her people,

as well as complimenting a loyal but unfortunate
servant. When her enemies thought her nearest
to ruin, then it was that Maria Theresa showed
herself so superior to fear that she infused her own
high courage into her army and her people. And for
this reason, when her military fortunes were low,
she chose rather to act as if disasters were mere
mishaps, to be redeemed in another campaign.

The Viennese, who love pageants better than
any other people in the world, were out early to
see the spectacle, which did not begin until ten
o'clock. Scarcely had the sun tipped the glorious
tower of the cathedral of St. Stephen, and blazoned
the long lines of windows in the Imperial Palace
until they shone like molten gold, before the streets
were thronged with citizens and people from the
surrounding country. The Empress Queen had
selected the broad and splendid plaza in front
of the Imperial Palace from which to view the
march past, and the multitudes poured toward the
Stadt, through the narrow and tortuous streets
which lead to this region of palaces, museums, and
churches. The morning was clear, mild, and beautiful, and the gay Viennese had apparently forgotten the dreadful day of Rosbach and the terrible
hours of Leuthen.

The sunny air resounded with martial music and the steady tread of marching feet of men and iron-shod hoofs of horses. Splendid coaches bearing ambassadors and ambassadresses rolled majestically through the streets. Great officers of state, resplendent in their orders and decorations, leaving their chariots wedged in the eager, curious, and noisy throng, made their way on foot to the palace doors. Military officers in glittering uniforms, with gorgeous horse trappings, dashed about on their spirited chargers. A blare of trumpets on the one hand was answered by the quick music of a military band on the other, and the air vibrated with the continuous clang of the fife and drum. It was the day of glory of the brave army, which, though defeated, stood ready to renew the conflict with its old enemy at the first signal. As the morning hours sped on toward ten o'clock the enthusiasm of the crowds increased. The prospect of seeing their Empress Queen in state always put the Viennese in a good humour, and the multitudes that packed the streets leading toward the palace were full of merriment and in the notion to be pleased with everything.

The approach of the troops was heralded with cheers that seemed to come from miles away, and followed them to the point where the head of the first column debouched before the palace. At the same moment a fanfare of silver trumpets from the trumpeters of the guard announced that the Empress Queen had left the palace. The great gates were thrown wide open, and the Imperial body-guard rode forth. This was a magnificent battalion of men, all mounted on coal-black horses, and wearing brass helmets and cuirasses that glittered in the dazzling light. After them came the Hungarian contingent, a people between whom and Maria Theresa a peculiar bond of affection subsisted. The people greeted these with imitations of the peculiarly wild and piercing cries of their country. Next rode the young archdukes, handsome lads, and superbly mounted. Last, appeared the Empress Queen, mounted upon a noble, iron-gray charger, with the Emperor Francis on her right and the Archduke Charles on her left.

Maria Theresa never looked more royal and imperial than when on horseback. She rode with exquisite grace, and her stately mien fitly indicated her brave spirit. Although then past her first youth and the mother of many children, she was still the most graceful princess in Europe; and maturity had not robbed her of her natural comeliness. Her

eyes still shone with star-like brightness, and the
colour mounted beautifully to her cheek when, after
a moment's sudden checking of noise, a roar of
joyous cheering, of wild hand-clapping, and of military music clashed heavenward. She had then ridden briskly out upon the open space, where, under
the splendid standards of the Empire, she bowed
right and left, with an enchanting smile. Maria
Theresa loved to be with her people, and was as
happy to show herself to them as they were pleased
to see her. The Emperor Francis, a handsome
man of middle age, and his brother, the Archduke
Charles, came in for their share of applause, and
acknowledged it gracefully. But the Empress
Queen had been for twenty years the darling of
the people, and her husband and children were
loved and applauded chiefly because they were hers.

The march past then began. First came a splendid body of cavalry, hussars, cuirassiers, and dragoons. The Hungarian contingent, led by their
hetmans, was gorgeously picturesque, and as they
waved their swords and lances in the air with wild
grace the Empress Queen responded with a charming inclination of the head. Maria Theresa had
not forgotten that in her most perilous hour the loyalty of the Hungarians had saved her throne and

country from the rapacity of Frederick. Next
came the foot regiments, sturdy men who had withstood the shock of battle, and whose stained and
tattered battle-flags showed what service they had
seen. The field artillery, then a great novelty in
warfare, followed, their long, bronze guns, cast
with the Empress Queen's crown and cipher in the
metal, gleaming dully in the sunlight. So brilliant
was the spectacle, that the hours sped away, and it
was long after noon when the end of the last column appeared in view.

Among those watching it, in the crowd of diplo-
mats, was a slight but singularly high-bred looking
man, evidently an Englishman. He sat in a plain
but handsome coach, magnificently horsed. All
who saw the parade and the outburst of affectionate
loyalty toward the Empress Queen were affected
to a certain degree by it except this English gentleman. He, however, regarded it all with a cool
smile, and did not speak except to make some disparaging remark to an officer in an English uniform who sat on horseback next the coach.

As the end of the columns drew near there was a
new and sudden outburst of cheering heard afar off,
mixed with laughter; the multitudes of people had
evidently seen something to both please and amuse

them. It was so noticeable that the Archduke Charles sent an aide riding down the line, who came back smiling. He approached the Empress Queen and the Emperor, and said something which caused them both to smile, too. At the same moment the last detachment of troops was passing, and directly behind them came a country cart, drawn by a sorry horse. On a plank laid across the cart sat Gavin Hamilton, driving. He still wore the enormous chapeau and cloak of General Kollnitz. The huge hat was pushed back, showing his handsome bronzed face, his white teeth gleaming in a perpetual smile; while he awkwardly held up the huge cloak in handling the coarse rope reins.

Sitting in solitary magnificence in the body of the cart was St. Arnaud, dressed in Pfels' hat and cloak. He sat flat, with his shapely legs stretched stiffly out before him, and, in contrast to Gavin's boyish grins of delight, St. Arnaud was as perfectly grave and composed as if in attendance upon royalty. The crowds had found out who they were, and shouts resounded, and cries were bandied about.

" There they are, in the disguise they escaped in! They say that Frederick was so angry when he heard of their getting away that he burst a blood-vessel! "

"And poor old Kollnitz took to his bed with chagrin, and has never left it since!" called out another.

The English gentleman turned to the officer on horseback and said:

"What children are these Viennese! Because a couple of officers make a clever escape, and appear riding in a cart, these childish people go wild with delight. Depend upon it, it is neither the escape nor the men who matter—it is the cart and horse which pleases them."

"You scarcely do the Viennese justice, Sir Gavin," replied the officer, standing up in his stirrups to look as the cart approached. "I recognize young St. Arnaud of Dufour's regiment as the officer sitting down; but who is the younger one—evidently St. Arnaud's junior—who is driving?"

Sir Gavin Hamilton stood up in the coach and looked attentively at the cart, which was then passing the royal party. Gavin brought the horse to a standstill, stood up, as did St. Arnaud, and both respectfully saluted the Empress Queen.

"That younger man," said Sir Gavin, with the utmost nonchalance, "is my son. He is not my heir, however."

The officer uttered an exclamation of surprise,

but Sir Gavin's face remained quite impassive. No one but the officer heard him, and the next moment there was a general movement of the privileged bystanders as the royal party turned toward the palace. Then an aide-de-camp rode up to the cart, and after a few words St. Arnaud and Gavin descended, and an orderly led the equipage away.

Gavin and St. Arnaud followed the aide, Captain Count Derschau, into the courtyard of the palace, and to a small door in a wing of the vast building. Entering, he showed them the way to a small anteroom, saying:

" You will remain here until Her Majesty sends for you, which will be within half an hour; " and courteously excusing himself, he left them.

CHAPTER VI

GAVIN and St. Arnaud remained in the little anteroom awaiting the summons to the Empress Queen. Gavin sat quite silent. A resolve that had taken possession of him filled his heart as well as his mind. He dared not mention it to St. Arnaud, for fear of his disapproval—and Gavin loved St. Arnaud so much that he could not bear to oppose him—but his resolution was unshakable. St. Arnaud, brought up in palaces and inured to royalty, yet felt something like agitation at meeting the celebrated woman whose courage and constancy had withstood the greatest captain of the age, Frederick of Prussia, for more than sixteen years. But he, too, remained silent, and in a short half hour the aide returned, and after leading them through a maze of splendid corridors and noble apartments, he showed them into a small and simply furnished room, where the Emperor Francis sat alone.

The Emperor rose at once; for it was the custom of Francis of Lorraine to observe a charming simplicity toward all with whom he was brought in contact. As consort of a great and popular sovereign in her own right, he chose rather to give her all precedence, and took but little ostensible share in the government. He adopted the rôle of the husband and father only, well knowing that the jealous and varied peoples composing the Austro-Hungarian empire would resent any open share in the government; and although the Empress Queen relied much on his excellent sense and judgment, she was herself the ruler of her people.

Gavin watched St. Arnaud's way of responding to the approaches of royalty, and followed him closely. There could have been no better example, as St. Arnaud, while perfectly respectful, was far from servile. The easy affability of the Emperor put them entirely at their ease, and in a few moments the door opened and the Empress Queen walked in.

The nearer view of Maria Theresa was still more pleasing and impressive than seeing her at a distance. Her commanding talents, and the lofty dignity which she naturally acquired as a reigning sovereign in her own right, were adorned by a beautiful feminine softness. The woman who was not afraid to face Frederick the Great, with his warrior army, was likewise gentle, considerate, and engaging.

Unlike Frederick, who valued men solely for their intellectual qualities, Maria Theresa trusted much to the excellence of their hearts, and, consequently, where one was feared, the other was loved.

The Emperor, who scrupulously observed the deference due his wife's rank, rose and remained standing until the Empress Queen had seated herself. Then turning to St. Arnaud, as the eldest, she said:

"I and the Emperor have been much pleased to hear of the escape of you and your brother officer from Glatz. I shall need every man who can carry a sword in the next campaign. Will you tell us the particulars of your capture? And meanwhile, pray be seated."

St. Arnaud promptly began his relation. He told the circumstances of Gavin and himself meeting after Rosbach, and was careful to say that but for that meeting he would have perished on that November night. He then described their going to the country house, their finding there a lady travelling with only a servant—Madame Ziska.

"Madame Ziska!" cried the Empress Queen,

turning to the Emperor. "No one has told me of this. You must know," she added, to St. Arnaud and Gavin, "that Madame Ziska is highly respected here, and I selected her on account of her good sense and discretion, as well as her accomplishments, to teach dancing to our children."

"We can testify, your Majesty, to her excellent heart as well as her admirable mind, for it was she who conveyed the money to us which made our escape possible," replied St. Arnaud.

He then described their evening with her, and the sudden appearance of the King of Prussia. At the mention of the name of her great enemy, Maria Theresa coloured deeply. She not only opposed Frederick as the enemy of her country, but she resented his conduct to her as a woman; and when that part of the narrative was reached in which St. Arnaud described Frederick's indifference to their fate next day, after their evening of jolly companionship, she smiled contemptuously.

But she smiled with the utmost graciousness when St. Arnaud said:

"We both refused the parole offered us, because we could not bring ourselves to accept any favour that would prevent us from drawing our swords in the service of your Majesty."

At this Gavin broke forth, his colour rising, his eyes moist, and his voice ringing with emotion:

"But, your Majesty, although I would fight for you to the last drop of my blood I have no sword to draw, unless you, out of your goodness, give me one; for I am but a private soldier. He "—pointing to St. Arnaud—" was too generous to tell it of me, but I was only a private in the ranks of Dufour's regiment, in which he was a captain. I am a gentleman, however, and I stand up and say to all the world I am not unworthy to wear an officer's sword in the army of any sovereign on earth!"

Gavin suddenly choked, and turning to St. Arnaud, cried:

"Tell it for me, St. Arnaud, for I cannot," and walked away to a window to hide his agitation.

St. Arnaud was somewhat disconcerted at Gavin's outbreak, but in response to a word of inquiry from the Empress Queen replied:

"What he says is true. He is the son of Sir Gavin Hamilton, who has ill-used him and his mother, and this young man was forced to take service in the ranks. But he is well educated, as your Majesty perceives by his language, and that he has the character and feelings of a gentleman is proved by his treatment of his father. For when Sir Gavin Hamilton offered him everything, provided he would abandon his mother, this youth refused, and chose rather poverty and obscurity than to cast dishonour upon his mother, who is Sir Gavin's true and lawful wife."

The Emperor, at this, said calmly:

"I heard only a few moments before you entered this room that the young man was Sir Gavin's son. Sir Gavin is at present in Vienna. Although England has left the ranks of our allies to join our enemies, yet, by mutual arrangement, citizens of one country are not obliged to leave the other until a fixed period. Sir Gavin has availed himself of this provision, and even appears at court as usual. I was told by Captain von Rosen that when you appeared riding in the cart at the end of the parade, Sir Gavin said to him: ' The younger man is my son, but not my heir.' I determined to inquire into the matter."

Gavin, at this, came from his retreat in the window, and cried:

" Sir Gavin might have said that to Baron von Rosen, but if he ever said so much to me, I would use my two fists on him as I did once before. For, your Majesty, such words are a reflection on my mother; and no man that lives, be he my father ten thousand times over, shall say one word against my mother without my doing him the worst injury I can in return for it. My mother is Lady Hamilton, and Sir Gavin admitted it when he threatened me with divorcing my mother, after having abandoned her many years ago. But I defied him to do it, and he dares not attempt it. Nor will my mother be driven or frightened into a divorce; for she is a brave lady, and will not do anything that may one day impair my rights or my standing."

The Empress Queen listened with shining eyes. To no one could an appeal to the feelings be made more safely than to Maria Theresa.

"How does life repeat itself!" she said. "Here is this mother, who holds tenaciously to her rights for her child's sake—for I believe every word you have told me. So do I hold on to all my rights, when the King of Prussia would ravage them from me, determined to transmit to my son his heritage unimpaired. Nor is it lost on me," she said, turning to Gavin, with the sweetest smile —" the son who is faithful to his mother in poverty and obscurity, rather than to the father in power and splendour. Therefore, you may look to me as a friend. You say you are a private soldier. Captain St. Arnaud says you are anxious to be an officer. Before this day is over you shall have a sublieutenant's commission in my army."

Gavin stood silent, stunned by his good fortune.

"And," added the Emperor, "I will give you the sword that her Majesty deems you worthy to wear."

Going to a cabinet in the room, he unlocked it, and revealed a number of handsome swords suitable for various occasions. Selecting one, a light but elegant blade, he handed it to the Empress Queen with much grace, saying:

"He will value it more from your hand."

The joy in Gavin's face when, dropping upon his knee, he received the sword from Maria Theresa transfigured him. It meant honour, glory, the recognition of his honourable birth—all of those things most precious to him and which had seemed so hopelessly far away. He kissed the hilt of the sword reverently as he received it, but he could not speak. He bowed low to the Emperor, and then suddenly turning to St. Arnaud—his happiness overcoming his usually acquired habits of restraint—and seizing him, kissed and hugged him violently.

This natural abandon, which would have offended many sovereigns, touched and also amused
the Empress Queen; and when Gavin recovered
himself, and stood, blushing and appalled at his
breach of etiquette, both Maria Theresa and the
Emperor Francis were laughing heartily. The
sight of Gavin's face, flushed and sparkling, his
mouth quivering, yet full of smiles, the boyish
dimples in his cheek showing, and his lithe, strong
body trembling with happiness, appealed to the
exquisitely human heart of Maria Theresa. She
saw in him a soul capable of the greatest devotion
to her.

"Your commission will be sent you to-day,
Lieutenant Hamilton," she said, with an air of the
utmost sweetness; "and you, Captain St. Arnaud,
will have your wishes fulfilled in any way possible."

Then, with a graceful bow of dismissal, she
rose from her chair. St. Arnaud, with a few appropriate words of gratitude, bowed himself out,
followed by Gavin. But before the door closed the
Empress Queen and the Emperor heard Gavin's
eager whisper, as he said:

"That noble queen and lady won't forget us
by to-morrow morning, as the King of Prussia

did; " which speech by no means hurt Gavin in the opinion of the imperial pair. Another person that heard him was Count Derschau, who awaited them outside the door.

St. Arnaud was well versed in courts, and foreseeing that Gavin would always be saying and doing unconventional things, he concluded to let the imperial circle understand that the Empress Queen and the Emperor were pleased with Gavin's *naïveté*—and when sovereigns are pleased, courtiers dare not find fault. He, therefore, began to tell, in his calm and easy manner, of Gavin's late behaviour, and their majesties' reception of it, at which Gavin blushed and Count Derschau shouted with laughter.

They were then passing along a gallery from which they could look down into a large, square room with a polished floor, where the royal children were assembled, with their governesses, for their dancing lesson. A couple of fiddlers were tuning up, when the door opened and in walked Madame Ziska.

Gavin was like to have leaped over the railing of the gallery in his delight and surprise at the unexpected meeting, and St. Arnaud said at once to Count Derschau:

114

"Would it be contrary to custom if we should speak to that lady who is entering? She is the one who assisted us so materially in our escape. We could not have got out without her."

"Certainly," responded Count Derschau. "You must know, monsieur, that this is a court where all that is natural and simple prevails. Besides the cares of empire, her Majesty has the welfare of her ten children at heart, as much as any house mother in her empire. The Emperor is the same; and so, although the Imperial Court does not, as you perceive, lack dignity, yet it is less trammelled by etiquette than any court in Europe. It is like one great family, of which the Empress Queen and Emperor are mother and father to us all."

Count Derschau led them down a stairway which opened upon the dancing-room, and advancing to the lady in charge of the royal children, presented St. Arnaud and Gavin, with the request that they might speak to Madame Ziska; to which she at once agreed.

Madame Ziska was at the end of the large room on her knees before the little two-year-old Arch-duchess Marie Antoinette, that lovely and most unfortunate princess, whose fair head was one day to fall beneath the axe of the guillotine. She was too young to be regularly taught to dance, but Madame Ziska, leading her by her tiny hand, and singing softly to her, she made little steps, and laughed in baby glee at her own performance.

But hearing familiar voices, Madame Ziska turned, and flying forward, the next moment she had grasped Gavin and St. Arnaud each by a hand, and was laughing and crying with pleasure at seeing them.

"Where should we have been without you!" cried Gavin, squeezing her hand with rapture.

"In the prison at Glatz, eating our miserable hearts out," answered St. Arnaud. "And the money—a hundred ducats—oh, what a fortune it was to us!"

"It was nothing, if it served to release two brave men to fight for the Empress Queen; for let me tell you, you must be hers, body and soul, as I am."

"We are—we are. Wait until we tell you of our interview with her Majesty just now," replied Gavin, with all his heart shining in his eyes.

"I long to speak with you," said Madame Ziska, "but I must now give the archdukes and archduchesses their dancing lesson. Come to my house —in the Teinfeltstrasse—you can easily find it—

at five o'clock, and remain to supper with my husband, my children, and me. We will talk all
night, that I promise you."

Making a low bow to the lady in charge, Madame Ziska then began her task, while Derschau,
with St. Arnaud and Gavin, withdrew.

"Madame Ziska is well known and highly respected in Vienna, as you may judge by her being
dancing mistress to the imperial children," said
Derschau. "She is also first dancer at the opera.
She is the wife of Count Kalenga, an Hungarian
nobleman. Ziska is only her stage name. He married her, to the ruin of his worldly prospects. He
was disinherited by his family for it, and Madame
Ziska's profession and her humble origin made it
impossible for her to be recognized in Viennese
society. Nevertheless, they lived very happily together upon the small remnant of his fortune that
remained to them until about four years ago.
Kalenga, who was one of the handsomest men in
the world, became a hopeless paralytic. Madame
Ziska, who has retained, as you see, her youth and
grace, returned to the stage, and by her own exer-
tions maintains her husband and family, giving
Kalenga all the comforts that his sad condition requires. The Empress Queen, who is herself the

best of wives and mothers, determined to encourage Madame Ziska by employing her as dancing mistress to the imperial children. As you see, although of humble birth, she is far superior to most of her profession. Her husband has educated her, and to-day she is one of the most accomplished women in Vienna."

"We know it," replied St. Arnaud. "Her conversation charmed the King of Prussia, and the tender, womanly interest she took in two strangers and prisoners showed that her sympathies were large enough to go beyond the narrow circle of her family."

They were then arrived at the small door of the palace by which they had entered, and Derschau bade them a courteous farewell, after engaging to receive the promised commission for Gavin, and keep it until he called for it next day.

Five o'clock found them before the door of a comfortable house in the Teinfeltstrasse. The door was opened by Madame Ziska herself, who led them to a pleasant room opening into a garden. Through the glass they could see Count Kalenga, muffled up, and sitting in a wheel-chair. Two handsome boys of ten and twelve were pushing the chair to a sheltered spot warmed by the last rays

of the setting sun, two younger girls leaning on
their father's lap; he was evidently telling them a
story, to which all four were listening. The scene
touched both Gavin and St. Arnaud, who knew
the story of the man so physically afflicted, but so
blessed with the devotion of a wife and children.

"Derschau has told you my story and my husband's, I know," said Madame Ziska good-humouredly. "He is a pleasant fellow, but a great
gossip—everybody knows everything that Derschau knows. But seeing my husband, even as he
is now"—she pointed to Count Kalenga, who was
being wheeled toward the house by the two boys—
and her soft eyes filled with tears, "are you surprised that a young and tender-hearted girl should
have married him? The time came when I re-
proached myself bitterly for having done it, after
I saw that it cost him his fortune and most of his
association with his equals. But if he ever regretted it, he was too noble to let me suspect it.
And when his affliction came upon him, could I
ever do enough to show my devotion to him? Ah,
do you wonder that I try to make myself his companion by reading, by studying—that every moment I spend away from him I grudge? Yet it is
sweetened by the thought that I am labouring for

him and our children. And at the opera, when the
idle young men throw me bouquets and write
verses to me, my only thought is, 'It will make
my husband smile'—it amuses him very much;
and when I find a jewel in a bouquet I very quickly exchange it for something to make his lot more
comfortable." She rose while she was speaking,
and opening the door, the chair was rolled in.

As Madame Ziska said, a view of her husband
made it quite plain why he won the heart of a
young and impressionable girl. His countenance,
still handsome, was full of candour and intelligence,
and his figure, in spite of his dreadful affliction,
retained its military uprightness. The little girls,
Gretchen and Freda, unfastened his cloak and removed his fur cap and gloves, while the lads, Franz
and Carl, well trained and polite, stood silent near
him, ready to be of service.

" You know who these friends are, Franz," said
Madame Ziska to Count Kalenga. St. Arnaud
and Gavin shook hands cordially with Kalenga,
who greeted them with the utmost grace and kindness. The children were then dismissed, and Madame Ziska, drawing her chair to the fire, said:

" Thank heaven I do not go to the opera to-
night. We will have supper here, and you shall

tell us all your adventures. But first, mother-like, I must see to your comfort. Have you lodgings yet ?"

" No, we have not thought of it yet."

" The floor above us is vacant, and is reasonable in price."

" If you say so, engage it for us. We will obey you as little Franz and Carl do."

" Very well. Now tell us all—all—all."

St. Arnaud and Gavin, both talking at once, plunged in and gave an account of all they had passed through since parting at the gates of Glatz on the moonlight night two months before. St. Arnaud told about Bettina's unflattering behaviour to them at separating, and Madame Ziska screamed with laughter, saying:

" I am glad my niece knows so well how to take care of herself; " to which Count Kalenga added, smiling:

" She has inherited some of my wife's spirit, for many times, when I was a presumptuous young officer, and she was the object of my devotion, I came perilously near having my ears boxed. I think, however," he continued, turning to Madame Ziska with an air of affectionate deference, " that all the women of your family have remarkable propriety of bearing, and exact respect from all."

Madame Ziska coloured with pleasure at this.

Supper was brought, and the whole party grew merry, even Kalenga. The enthusiasm with which the Empress Queen had filled St. Arnaud and Gavin was deeply gratifying to their hosts, and Gavin's solemn promise that the sword given him by Maria Theresa was forever at the service of her and her family, was but a just acknowledgment of his obligations to her.

" You should have seen her as I did, at Presburg, in 1741, when she won the hearts of all Hungarians," said Kalenga, leaning forward in his chair, his eyes sparkling, and his hand involuntarily reaching for the sword, no longer at his side, that he had worn so many years in the service of the Empress Queen. " She was then but twenty-four years old, and the handsomest woman of her time. On the day of her coronation, when she rode gallantly up the Sacred Mount wearing the tattered robe of St. Stephen over her splendid habit, the iron crown of St. Stephen on her head, and, drawing St. Stephen's sword, defied the four corners of the earth, she was sovereign of the hearts of all who saw her. But greater still was she when she entered the Hall of the Diet, wearing the Hungarian dress, in deep mourning,

and the same crown and sword of St. Stephen.
Never can any who lived that hour of glorious
patriotism forget it. She was the picture of
majesty, fearless and unappalled, when, standing upon her throne, she recounted to us, the assembled nobles of Hungary, all the dangers that
menaced her, and her sole defence lay in the
loyalty and generosity of her Hungarian people.
The King of Prussia, when he attacked her kingdom, openly counted upon her timidity as a young
and inexperienced princess. Young and inexperienced she was—but no man ever made so
great a mistake as Frederick when he reckoned
upon the timidity of Maria Theresa. She had
ever the courage of a hundred kings in her woman's heart. So did she inspire us on that never-
to-be-forgotten day, that as one man we rose, and
with shouts and cheers and clanging of our swords,
as we drew them half way from their scabbards
and sent them ringing back again, cried: ' We will
die for our King, Maria Theresa.' At that, the
woman's heart, which ever dwells in her, made
itself felt. She, who had scorned fear when the
men around her trembled, and who proposed to
die rather than yield to injustice, burst into tears,
and wept before us. Oh, then we were wild—we

wept, too—but they were tears of love and admiration and devotion to her who was so much a queen and yet so much a woman. And from that day to this has she been the darling of the Hungarian people!"

"And she is worthy of it!" cried St. Arnaud, roused from his habitual calm, and speaking before Gavin had time to take breath after Kalenga's recital. Madame Ziska supplemented her husband's glowing words by many stories of the Empress Queen's excellence as a wife and mother, and Gavin and St. Arnaud were eager listeners. Gavin was ready to believe anything of the courage and nobility of a woman defending her rights —he had seen an example of it in his own mother. St. Arnaud, familiar with a corrupt court, where evil and designing women held empire, was glad to know that a royal and imperial lady could make virtue fashionable and decorum popular.

"And now," said Madame Ziska after a while, "let us go upstairs and see the apartment that I wish our landlord to let to you."

Taking candles, she led them upstairs, where, above her, was a comfortable suite of rooms to be had. Gavin, in the impetuosity of his gratitude and affection for Madame Ziska, would have leased a dog-kennel recommended by her. St. Arnaud, cooler and more experienced, saw that the rooms were really desirable, and that Madame Ziska was a good counsellor in the every-day affairs of life. Gavin declared that he meant to stay that very night, as they had no other lodgings, and it was not likely the landlord would come and turn them out. St. Arnaud laughingly agreed; Madame Ziska abetted them by lending them sheets and pillows, and at midnight they tumbled into bed and slept the sleep of the just, untroubled by any qualms as trespassers.

Next morning, by ten o'clock, they had engaged the lodgings. But earlier even than that Gavin had gone after his commission, and had received with it a small sum of money, by way of pay, in advance. It was modest enough, but it was more money than Gavin had ever seen at any one time in his life. With it he could pay back his part of Madame Ziska's loan and fit himself out with clothes and uniforms. St. Arnaud could draw, in Vienna, on his funds in Paris—so they could establish themselves in comfort in their new quarters, which they proceeded to do. The proudest moment of Gavin's life was when he stood up to be measured for his uniform in the hussar regiment to which he had been assigned. It was approached, however, by the joy he felt in signing his name to a long letter to his mother—" Your affectionate son, Gavin Hamilton, sublieutenant in the Jascinsky Regiment of Hussars of her Imperial Majesty, the Empress Queen Maria Theresa."

It is not often that any human being enjoys perfect happiness, even for a single day; but for a time it fell to Gavin Hamilton's fortunate lot. It is true, he felt it necessary to his credit, as well as his happiness, that his mother should be redeemed from her life of toil, and he ardently longed to have her with him. This, however, he knew to be practicable, and with his sanguine temperament, he regarded it as already accomplished. And so it was a time of happiness that he entered upon at Vienna, the memory of which was a joy to him as long as he lived. Within the week he had completed the formalities necessary to receive his commission, and he was to attend the Empress Queen's levee, to "kiss hands" upon entering the royal service. St. Arnaud was also to go, to pay his formal respects at court. The levee was held in the evening, and Madame Ziska, who danced at the opera that night, actually drove home, in the intervals of the performance, to see

her two friends. St. Arnaud, who had recovered
his good looks, along with regularity in having
something to eat, and fresh air and exercise, was
exquisitely handsome in his new and dazzling uniform. Gavin, who had no regular beauty, but a
fine figure and a frank, speaking face, looked his
best in his white hussar jacket and glittering
accoutrements. No mother admiring her young
daughters dressed for their first ball could have
shown more pride and pleasure than Madame Ziska. The children, who were allowed to stay up
as a special privilege, were in raptures of delight,
while even Kalenga, who was always patient, but
seldom gay, smiled in sympathy with the pleasure
of those around him. At last St. Arnaud and
Gavin set off in a hired coach.

A great crowd of notabilities filled the ante-
rooms of the palace, but way was made everywhere
for Gavin and St. Arnaud. Their story had been
told broadcast in Vienna, and the proudest and
most exclusive society in Europe was prepared to
welcome them. St. Arnaud was already well
known, and Gavin's relationship to the haughty
and unpopular Sir Gavin Hamilton was public
property. St. Arnaud had remarked to Gavin,
on entering the palace:

" Surely Sir Gavin Hamilton will absent himself from this levee. He will not wish to be brought face to face with you."

" You little know my father," replied Gavin. " It is not in him to avoid anybody or anything. This much I must say of him—he does not know how to skulk."

True as Gavin had said. As they reached the door of the imperial apartments, Sir Gavin Hamilton, plainly but elegantly dressed, and wearing a diamond-hilted sword and a single splendid decoration on his breast, barred the way. He was conversing with the Chancellor, the celebrated Prince Kaunitz, known as " the coach driver of Europe," from his superior management of affairs. Great as Kaunitz was, he had an obtrusive vanity, amazing in a man of so much power and ability. In contrast to Sir Gavin Hamilton's studied simplicity of attire, Kaunitz was a mass of jewels and embroidery, while the entire breast of his blue velvet coat was covered with medals, orders, and decorations. Sir Gavin, a single eyeglass in his eye, surveyed the Chancellor with cool arrogance, and even the mighty Kaunitz was impressed by the calm assurance of the English baronet.

Sir Gavin directly blocked the doorway, and after waiting a few moments, Gavin, exchanging glances with St. Arnaud, tapped Sir Gavin on the arm lightly, and said:

" Pardon, but will you kindly permit us to enter ? "

Sir Gavin turned around, without making way in the least, and quietly surveyed his son for a whole minute.

" I asked," said Gavin, slightly raising his voice, " if ¯you would kindly permit us to enter."

The little scene had attracted the attention of those near by, and it was perfectly well known who Gavin was. Kaunitz, who heartily disliked Sir Gavin, watched with a sly smile the outcome of this novel encounter, and anxiously hoped for the baronet's discomfiture.

Gavin met Sir Gavin's cold, impassive glance with one full of a steady defiance. They were very unlike, this father and son—Sir Gavin, small, slight, and pale, and Gavin, tall and well developed for his twenty years; but when they stood face to face, defying each other, as it were, a strange likeness came out between them—no one could doubt then their relationship.

After a moment more Gavin coolly unbuckled his sword, and handing it to St. Arnaud, said:

" The Empress Queen gave me that sword with her own hand; therefore, it shall touch no unworthy thing." And as quick as a flash he seized Sir Gavin around the waist, and setting him aside, as if he were a chair, or any other piece of light furniture, walked in, followed by St. Arnaud, who handed him his sword.

There was a burst of suppressed laughter, in which Kaunitz's delighted cackle could be heard. Sir Gavin, pale with rage, was yet indomitable, and looked about him with an unabashed front. Kaunitz, whose opportunity it was, sauntered up, smiling blandly.

" My dear Sir Gavin, I feel the utmost sympathy for you. Most disrespectful of *your son.*"

" Yes, he is my son," slowly replied Sir Gavin, " but—"

Gavin, a few steps farther on, turned back, his face as pale as his father's.

" Be guarded in what you say," he said in a distinct voice.

" But not my heir," continued Sir Gavin.

Gavin made one swift and silent step toward him. Close at hand was an open window, and

" HE DROPPED SIR GAVIN ON TO THE FLOWER-BED FIFTEEN FEET BELOW "

out of it Gavin instantly handed Sir Gavin, holding him carefully suspended, and dropping him considerately upon a flower-bed fifteen feet below.

" I have not hurt him," he said, turning to the astonished spectators. " I have let him down very softly. You see, I cannot let any one, least of all my father, Sir Gavin Hamilton, say that of me, because it reflects upon my mother. And I dare not wear the sword given me by the Empress Queen, nor even face her Majesty, if I suffer one disrespectful word to be spoken of my mother, Lady Hamilton."

There was a ripple of applause and laughter. All had occurred so quickly and quietly that only those immediately around them in the vast anteroom knew anything of what had happened. But it spread rapidly. St. Arnaud drew Gavin away, whose face was now deeply flushed, and who was beginning to show agitation.

" I do not know whether this will be my ruin or not with the Empress Queen," he said in an excited whisper to St. Arnaud; " I only know that some force stronger than I, and better, too, than I, impels me to defend my mother's good name whenever this man attacks it; and if ruin comes because of it, let it come. Had Sir Gavin been standing on the very steps of the throne, I should have done as I did."

"You are quite right; you have nothing to fear. Prince Kaunitz saw it all, and you may be sure that the right account will get to the Emperor and Empress Queen. So let us take our places in line as if nothing had occurred," counselled St. Arnaud.

This they proceeded to do, and in their turn they entered the splendid apartment, where weekly the imperial levee was held. On a daïs under a canopy of crimson velvet sat Maria Theresa and the Emperor Francis. The Empress Queen, in a white gown, with a crimson velvet mantle lightly thrown across her shoulders, wearing superb jewels, and a small tiara on her dark hair, was a picture of matronly beauty. No one would have suspected that this majestic and serene woman often spent nights of agonized weeping over her lost armies at Rosbach and Leuthen. Misfortune might rend her heart, but it could not shake her lofty spirit, and she set an heroic example of hope and courage. She was talking affably to those about her, especially a very old man, in the dress of an Hungarian magnate, for whom she had caused a chair to be placed, in consideration of his infirmities. As each person was presented she had an appropriate word, and when St. Arnaud's time came, she acknowledged his respectful greeting by saying pleasantly:

"I desire to hear more of your adventures in getting out of Glatz."

To Gavin she said that which gave him a thrill of the deepest happiness.

"I hope, Lieutenant Hamilton, that you have informed your mother, Lady Hamilton, of your fortunate escape."

CHAPTER VII

DURING the winter of 1758 Vienna society found one of its most interesting subjects of small talk in the affairs of Sir Gavin Hamilton and his son, Lieutenant Gavin Hamilton, of the Jascinsky Regiment of Hussars. Of course, all sorts of variations were given to the story, the plain, unvarnished truth being the version seldomest heard and least believed. Although England had withdrawn from her alliance with the Empress Queen, and the King of Prussia had secured an English alliance and an English subsidy of nearly seven hundred thousand pounds, it was the policy of Kaunitz to treat the English in Vienna in a conciliatory manner. There were only a few of them, chiefly gentlemen of fortune like Sir Gavin Hamilton, who had a fancy for what was then, next to Paris, the gayest city of continental Europe, and who took advantage of the permission to remain until the actual outbreak of hostilities in the spring. Nowhere was the spirit of resistance to

Frederick's aggressions so determined as in Vienna, and it was the belief both of the great Chancellor and his imperial mistress that it would be well for Englishmen of rank and standing to note the undaunted front with which the Court of Vienna met misfortunes, and prepared to redeem them. Sir Gavin was distinctly unpopular; but that, which would have been a reason with most men for leaving Vienna at the earliest feasible moment, was reason enough to keep him there until the last possible hour. He had an unshakable self-possession, and it gave him a cynical amusement to show himself when the world expected him to take himself off; to smile and be at his ease when other men would have been miserably ill at ease; to calmly ignore the attitude of others when it did not coincide with his own attitude. He appeared punctually at the next weekly levee of the Empress Queen, after he had been dropped out of the window by his son, and bore with perfect composure the sly smiles and covert gibes to which his adventure gave rise. Only on one point did he change. Twice had he met Gavin, and each time the slur cast upon Lady Hamilton had been resented in a way against which he was practically defenceless. All the sneers and jeers in the world were helpless against a young man with such fine, powerful arms and legs as Gavin's, and who had no scruple whatever in using them. Sir Gavin saw, therefore, the absolute impossibility of conveying any slight upon Lady Hamilton in her son's presence without being made not only odious, but ridiculous; and, like Gavin, he knew perfectly well that no place and no company would give him security, when the occasion rose, from the just resentment of the son of the woman he had so injured.

Gavin, deep in learning the duties of his new position, yet lost not a moment in trying to get his mother to Vienna. The journey would be long and expensive, and it would require rigid economy for both of them to live on his hussar's pay; yet his affectionate heart yearned to have her with him. Madame Ziska and her husband, and St. Arnaud, who knew the world well, pointed out other reasons why it was desirable that Lady Hamilton should come to Vienna.

"It is your great opportunity," said St. Arnaud one evening when they all sat together in Madame Ziska's apartment. "There is no doubt that the Empress Queen will receive your mother as Lady Hamilton, and it will carry great weight in your contest for your rights."

"Especially will it be so," added Kalenga, who was a man of much sense, "if she is received as Lady Hamilton while Sir Gavin Hamilton is here. It will be plain that there could be no deception about it, and that the Empress Queen knew the exact status of the case. Therefore, I recommend you to make every effort and every sacrifice to get your mother to you at the earliest moment. When the campaign opens in the spring, you will be obliged to leave Vienna. You should have her here before you are ordered away."

"And I," said St. Arnaud, "through my connections in France, can arrange for her to start and have money advanced to her."

"And I," chimed in Madame Ziska, "can lend you a few ducats to help her out."

The ever-ready tears filled Gavin's eyes.

"Why should I have such friends? I think it must be my mother's blessing that brings them. But, oh, me! I do not know where in Paris my mother can now be found. The last letter that reached me was in the summer. She may have changed her quarters since then."

"Never mind," cried St. Arnaud encouragingly. "It is not likely that she did not take steps to have her whereabouts known, and the King's police can find her, anyhow."

That very night St. Arnaud wrote a packet of letters, to be dispatched by the next post to France. Only after they were gone did he tell Gavin that he had directed his friends in Paris, not only to find Lady Hamilton, but to supply her with everything needful for her comfort in making the long journey. More than that, he went next day to Prince Kaunitz, and laying before him the facts in the case, got a specific promise from him that the Empress Queen would receive Lady Hamilton on her arrival. And he and Gavin, in whatever company they found themselves, took pains to announce the coming arrival of Lady Hamilton. The presence of Sir Gavin made a very pretty complication, and conjecture ran riot in Vienna society as to what he would say and do when the catastrophe came. Sir Gavin discounted it all by saying and doing nothing whatever. Bets were freely made as to the date when Sir Gavin would be driven to flight. The Chancellor, Kaunitz, hearing it talked of one evening in the Empress Queen's antechamber, took a pinch of snuff, and coolly poising it between his thumb and forefinger, remarked:

"Sir Gavin Hamilton will remain in Vienna as long as he is not wanted. The day we appear to wish him to stay he will take post for Berlin or London or the devil. Yesterday I achieved the greatest diplomatic stroke of my career. Sir Gavin came to see me at the Chancellery, and inquired whether he could have permission to remain in Vienna, if he so desired, beyond the time stipulated in his passport. I was on the alert at once. I knew, whatever he supposed my wishes were, that would he not do. Therefore, I answered him in such a manner that he did not and cannot find out whether his presence here is pleasing or displeasing to her Imperial Majesty's government. That is what I call a diplomatic triumph."

And Kaunitz dramatically waved his jewelled hand and lace-trimmed handkerchief in the air.

"But the wife he repudiates is coming," suggested a pert maid of honour. Kaunitz shook his head.

"No such trifle as that, my dear lady, will move Sir Gavin Hamilton. Englishmen are obstinate, but Sir Gavin Hamilton has an obstinacy as tall and as wide and as deep as the cathedral of St. Stephen."

On a snowy day in February, about the time

139

that Lady Hamilton was expected, St. Arnaud sat
alone in his apartment. He was hard at work
over some details of his regiment; for the remnants of it had been got together, and with the
new recruits it could make a tolerable showing
in numbers. Below he could hear the Kalenga
children romping—Madame Ziska was away at the
palace giving the dancing lesson to the little archdukes and archduchesses, and Kalenga, the most
devoted of fathers, allowed his children much
more indulgence than their mother. They grew
so noisy presently that when St. Arnaud heard the
grinding of wheels before the door, he said to himself:

"Thank heaven, Madame Ziska is come, and
they will now be quiet."

But, looking out of the window, he saw it was
not Madame Ziska who was descending from the
carriage, but a lady in black, whose slightness and
youthfulness of figure made it seem impossible
that she should be the mother of a son as old as
Gavin Hamilton.

St. Arnaud returned to his work, until he heard
steps ascending the stairs, and Freda's childish
voice saying:

"The gentlemen are out, but I can show you to

Lieutenant Gavin's room—that is what we call him."

The door opened and Lady Hamilton entered. The youthfulness of her figure was not fulfilled in her face. Sorrow and want had done their work there; they had clouded, though not destroyed her delicate beauty. Her dark eyes were Gavin's eyes, but her hair, once a deep brown, was plentifully streaked with gray. Her complexion, extremely fair, had not the red glow of youth, and her fine, straight features were thin and marked. But however much she had the signs of having suffered, she was now palpitating with joy, and her pallor was that of overpowering emotion. Her eyes rested upon St. Arnaud, then quickly searched the room.

"He is not here—my son—" she said, trembling as she spoke.

"No, madam," replied St. Arnaud, rising, "but he will be here very shortly."

Lady Hamilton advanced to the middle of the room, and placing her hand on St. Arnaud's arm, said:

"I know well who you are—my son's friend and best benefactor. I am almost glad that Gavin is not here, for I did not know how much it would agitate me to meet him."

St. Arnaud led her tenderly to a chair, saying:
" Remember, you are among friends who honour you and love Gavin."

The woman, who had borne with stoical composure for twenty years the miseries of a repudiated wife, broke down under these words of kindness. She laid her head upon her arms and sobbed convulsively. Freda, with wide and frightened childish eyes, watched her, while St. Arnaud let her weep unchecked; he saw that it was doing her good. Freda, who was an affectionate child, stole her little hand in Lady Hamilton's, and asked earnestly:

" Won't you let me get you some coffee to make you stop crying—and a little piece of bread with it and some cheese ? "

Lady Hamilton drew the child to her, and smiling through her tears, called her a dear child. Freda thought the ways of grown people very remarkable.

In a few minutes Lady Hamilton recovered her self-possession—the pains of joy are short-lived—and sat up, her wan face glowing with happiness. And then, just as she and St. Arnaud were talking as if they had known each other forty years, an eager step was heard on the stairs, and Gavin, his face flushed with exercise, and looking every inch a man and a soldier in his hussar uniform, bounded into the room. St. Arnaud slipped into his own bedroom—the meeting between the mother and son was too sacred for other eyes.

Gavin caught his mother in his arms and strained her to his heart. Both wept—they had shed no tears at parting—and a dozen times Gavin cried: "Mother! my mother!" and Lady Hamilton answered: "My son! my excellent, brave son," as if the mere repetition of the title each loved gave them joy.

The first rapturous kisses over, mother and son looked at each other with new eyes. When they had parted nearly two years before, Gavin was a boy. He had looked up to his mother for help in every relation of life, and she had been forgetful, as mothers are, of the development of the boy into the man, and had yearned over him in his youth and inexperience much as she had watched over him in his cradle. Now, in the twinkling of an eye, after a separation of two years, their situations were reversed. The mother saw at one glance that here she had a stay and prop—the days of her comfort were beginning. And the son saw that, in the natural evolution of events, he could now begin to return to his mother that all-providing care with which she had sheltered his hard and poverty-stricken youth. Lady Hamilton surveyed his tall and well-formed figure with delight. She had never before in her life seen him tolerably well dressed. To keep him decent had taxed all her slender resources; and to see him in all the splendour of his white hussar uniform was a revelation to her.

"I did not know you were so nearly handsome," she said fondly, kissing his forehead. "But I never before saw you in the guise of a gentleman."

"Oh, my mother," cried Gavin, "after I had left you and knew something of the world, I wondered how you, alone and forsaken in a strange country, ever continued to live at all! And to feed and clothe *me*—what a burden I must have been to you!"

"No burden, but my only joy and hope. Tell me, therefore, my son, have you so lived since we parted that I can still have joy and hope in you? Look me in the face and tell me if you have led a clean life and an upright life, for I know you cannot deceive my eyes, even if you would."

Gavin looked at her honestly, clearly, unflinchingly.

"I have not been perfect, mother," he replied. "No one is that, you have always told me; but there is not one hour of my life since we parted that you cannot know all about, if you wish to hear it. Remember, the ways and talk of private soldiers, of whom I was one for two years, are not the ways and talk in which you bred me; but these soldiers were honest, brave fellows, if they were uncouth and coarse. I have felt, however, much more at home in the company which St. Arnaud made possible to me than I ever did among the soldiers; and in one thing, at least, I obeyed your commands"—here Gavin laughed— "I was often ragged and always cold and hungry, but I never was a moment without a piece of soap, a comb, and a razor."

At which Lady Hamilton smiled and said:

"You are my own true boy. My father and my brothers were always clean and well-shaven, as becomes gentlemen. I don't know how I should feel toward a son who neglected those things."

Gavin grew serious enough the next moment, for he said:

"And do you know that my—that Sir Gavin Hamilton is in Vienna?"

A deep flush rose instantly in Lady Hamilton's

pale face. Gavin went on and described his adventure with Sir Gavin Hamilton at the imperial palace and everything connected with him, and especially the possibility that he and Lady Hamilton might meet if Lady Hamilton went to the Empress Queen's levee, which she, no doubt, would.

" And after her Majesty receives you, mother," cried Gavin exultingly, " Sir Gavin can no longer insult you by saying you were not his wife."

" But will her Majesty receive me ? "

" Undoubtedly; so Prince Kaunitz has promised St. Arnaud. And I have privately told St. Arnaud that if by any accident or intrigue it is refused, or even delayed, I will resign my commission at once and enlist again as a private soldier. But St. Arnaud will manage it. St. Arnaud has a great family connection in Paris. The Chancellor, Kaunitz, knows all about him—so trust St. Arnaud to do for you what he has done for me. He is the best friend with whom mortal man was ever blessed."

" I long to see him again. When I arrived I was so overcome and agitated that I scarcely knew what I was saying; but I loved him before I ever saw him. And I love that good Madame Ziska—

ah, Gavin, Gavin, how much good there is in the world!"

"Come," cried Gavin, jumping up. "I hear the carriage at the door—Madame Ziska has returned from the opera-house—and where is St. Arnaud?"

Gavin ran in the other rooms of the apartment, shouting:

"St. Arnaud! Where are you? Come and see my mother;" but St. Arnaud was nowhere to be found. Gavin then escorted his mother to the floor below to meet Madame Ziska and her husband. In all the terrible privations, humiliations, and struggles of twenty years, Lady Hamilton had never lost the best part of her birthright—the air and manner of the high-bred Englishwoman. Her black gown was shabby and her slim hands roughened by the actual toil she had been compelled to do, but she was everywhere at ease, with that serene and graceful unconsciousness which is the mark of a person born to consideration. Madame Ziska, although born and bred in a far humbler position in life than the English gentlewoman, had been gifted with a natural refinement and good sense that was equal to all the advantages of birth and early education; so the two women, on meeting, had every reason to be mutually satisfied with the other.

Gavin very proudly introduced his mother as " Lady Ameeltone "—for he had not yet learned the true pronunciation of his own name—to Madame Ziska and Count Kalenga. Lady Hamilton took both of Madame Ziska's hands in hers and said earnestly:

" How can I thank you enough for what you have done for my son ? "

To which Madame Ziska replied in her more emotional and demonstrative way:

" Oh, madam, he is such a nice lad! And when I saw those two admirable young men that freezing night when we first met, my heart went out to them. At first they did not know whether I was married or a widow. I believe they thought at first I was a widow, they paid me so many gallant compliments, and all the time I was laughing to myself, thinking how their tone would change if they knew I had a husband and four big children snugly tucked away at home."

" True," cried Gavin with a grin. " We were sure that Madame Ziska was a young widow, she was so charming, and we felt quite flat when we found she regarded us merely as a couple

of schoolboys to be helped out of a predica-
ment."

Kalenga then joined in the conversation, and
the children were brought in and presented, Freda
especially, a pretty, quaint child of thirteen, who
had already made friends with Lady Hamilton.
When Madame Ziska addressed her as Lady Hamilton, she smiled sadly and said:

"A title has often seemed a mockery to me,
when I have been in so great poverty and obscurity
for so many years. But it is a part of my son's
heritage, and that is why I hold to it."

Madame Ziska, the soul of hospitality, proposed
that they should all sup together.

"And how vexatious it will be of St. Arnaud if
he is not here," she said. "He must be detained
somewhere. As I do not dance to-night, we can
put off our supper until eight o'clock, and by that
time he will probably be here."

The afternoon passed only too quickly, Lady
Hamilton listening to the adventures of Gavin,
and every moment feeling a deeper thankfulness
for the man he had become. She herself, accustomed in her youth to the most refined society,
had formerly noted with regret many little things
in Gavin which it was inevitable that he should

acquire from the humble associates of his childhood and boyhood. But all these small faults of manners and language seemed to have disappeared. In two short months Gavin had become perfectly fitted for the society to which he was born and entitled.

Eight o'clock came, and Kalenga's chair had just been wheeled up to the comfortable supper-table, when St. Arnaud appeared. Madame Ziska covered him with reproaches for deserting them on that, of all afternoons.

"Wait, madam," mysteriously said St. Arnaud. "I have not been forgetful of Lady Hamilton, though I presume she thought I vanished into thin air when I disappeared so suddenly. I have been to see Prince Kaunitz at the Chancellery. The Chancellor has been to see the Empress Queen, and has just given me this."

St. Arnaud drew from his pocket an elaborately sealed letter, with the imperial arms, addressed to "The Lady Hamilton." It was a letter from the Court Chamberlain commanding the attendance of Lady Hamilton at the next weekly levee of the Empress Queen, on the following Tuesday evening.

Gavin jumped up, snapped his fingers, danced, laughed, embraced St. Arnaud a dozen times.

150

"Now," he cried, "we will see what Sir Garvan Ameeltone"—with infinite contempt—"will do when her Majesty receives Lady Ameeltone!"

Lady Hamilton, more accustomed than Gavin to the society of the great, was deeply gratified, but not, like him, highly elated; and when he spoke of his father in a tone that indicated so much hatred and contempt, she flashed him a look that reduced him to silence at once. Nevertheless, there was no mistaking the earnest gratitude of the few words, straight from her heart, with which she thanked St. Arnaud. It was, indeed, a long step toward her rights to be received by a great and virtuous sovereign in the very presence, as it were, of the man who had vainly tried to repudiate her.

It was an evening of great happiness to them all. Madame Ziska and Kalenga had become so attached to Gavin and St. Arnaud that whatever made them happy, the husband and wife shared thoroughly. Lady Hamilton found in Kalenga so much patience under misfortune, and so much affection and appreciation of his wife, that she honoured him with all her heart. When she saw their mutual devotion, she could not but think with vain regret: "Had Sir Gavin Hamilton so treated me, I should have been the happiest woman in the world."

Next morning a very great and important subject came up, of which only Lady Hamilton and Madame Ziska realized the true significance. This was the gown that Lady Hamilton was to wear to the imperial levee. Gavin tried to settle it at once by saying:

" Go to the shops and buy the handsomest gown you can find. I can pay for a part of it, and St. Arnaud will lend me the rest."

" Thank you, no," replied his mother, smiling. " It would not be in good taste that I should appear handsomely dressed, even if you had the money, which you have not. It is much better that my dress should be as simple as circumstances will allow. Therefore, I shall wear a plain black satin gown. When I was presented, in my girlhood, to the King and Queen of England, I wore a very simple gown, for my parents were not rich people for their station in life. I think I cannot do better than follow their plan now, although they have long since been taken from me."

The days could not go fast enough for Gavin between then and Tuesday. The only thing that marred his happiness was the possibility that Sir

Gavin Hamilton would not be present to witness the triumph of the woman he had so ill used and insulted. True, Sir Gavin did not mean to be at the levee, for he heard in due time of the arrival of his wife, and knew that the Empress Queen would receive her. But he had no notion of being driven from Vienna by her presence, and sardonically concluded that Lady Hamilton would be as anxious to avoid him as he would be to avoid her.

Tuesday evening came, and Gavin and St. Arnaud, dressed in their court uniforms, awaited Lady Hamilton's appearance from her room. With only little Freda to assist her, Lady Hamilton was making her toilet. Presently the door opened, and Freda, with a candle in each hand, came out, looking solemn beyond expression, and putting the candlesticks on the table, gazed with grave admiration at Lady Hamilton, who followed her.

Gavin caught his breath with admiration when his mother came full into the circle of light. He had never thought of her as a beautiful woman, only as the dearest woman in the world. He had seen only in her large, dark eyes the mother love shining for him. He had only felt in her rare smiles the sympathy with him that made her smile sometimes in the midst of her hard lot. And he had never seen her dressed except in the plainest and, often, in the shabbiest manner.

But to-night she wore her simple black satin robe with the air of a princess. For the first time in twenty years her beautiful white neck and handsome arms were bared to view. Her hair, silver and black mingled, was still abundant, and arranged with singular grace and becomingness. At night the lines of care in her face were not visible; pleasure, from which she had long since parted, had again come to her, and had brought to her cheek a flush like the glow of youth. She wore no jewels—she had none to wear—but her majestic and high-bred beauty needed no ornaments.

Gavin's first gasp of admiration over, he was strangely silent, while St. Arnaud, with the polished grace of a man of the world, complimented Lady Hamilton upon her distinguished appearance. No woman ever loses her appreciation of a pretty compliment, and as for Gavin, Lady Hamilton was more touched than she would have acknowledged by his admiration. She had asked herself while dressing: " Will he like me in this guise?" as a young girl questions of her lover. There was no doubt that Gavin liked her in that guise; but when his mother turned to him once more his eyes were full of tears.

"Oh, my mother," he cried. "To think what youth and beauty were yours when sorrow came to you! To think that I, your child, never before saw you except in the clothes of work and poverty! I feel now as I never felt before the terrible hardship of your lot."

"But the worst is over," replied Lady Hamilton; "and remember, I always had you."

"Yes, to feed and clothe; to eat up all you could earn; to wear out the poor garments you could afford to buy me."

"At least, all you had was honestly earned. Let us be thankful that you lived at no man's grudging table and wore no one's cast-offs. That is why, after so many years of work and poverty, we are still able to take our stand among our equals."

As Lady Hamilton spoke with so much spirit and dignity, it occurred to St. Arnaud that the man who could desert such a woman must be very perverse or very bad.

St. Arnaud handed Lady Hamilton into the hired carriage that was to take her and Gavin to the palace, saying he would follow them as soon as he could dispose of some letters he must have ready for the next post to Paris.

As Lady Hamilton and Gavin walked together through the splendid saloons of the Imperial Court none there showed more dignity and composure. Lady Hamilton was the only woman present who wore no jewels, and this absence of ornament made her conspicuous. She was, however, well fitted by her splendid dignity and the calm and unruffled manner of an English gentlewoman to stand the scrutiny of the hundreds of eyes levelled at her. The universal verdict was the same as St. Arnaud's in respect to Sir Gavin Hamilton. Gavin, resplendent in his gorgeous, white uniform, looked about him with sparkling eyes of triumph, which said plainly to all: " This is my mother. Have I not a right to be proud of her ? " Many persons stopped and spoke with them while they were finding their place in line. Among them was Prince Kaunitz. The Chancellor ever had an eye to grace and dignity in a woman, and within a few minutes of being presented to Lady Hamilton he whispered to her and Gavin:

" Will you do me the honour to sup at my house after the levee ? "

Lady Hamilton accepted with politeness, and
Gavin with a frank delight he could not conceal.
These little supper parties at the Chancellor's
house were among the most agreeable and distinguished parties in Vienna. Only a small number
of persons, more eminent for talents than rank,
and the best among the foreign visitors at Vienna,
were asked to them. To be invited once gave the
entrée to any of them. Gavin had never been bid-
den before, and he knew very well that he was
indebted to his mother's personal charm for being
invited at all.

When their turn came to be ushered into the
presence of the Empress Queen, Lady Hamilton
showed to great advantage. Unabashed by Maria
Theresa's splendid presence, she, nevertheless, did
homage to so much greatness united with all the
attractions of a charming and lovable woman.
The Empress Queen's first remark was to say,
with slight but unmistakable emphasis on the
words, " Lady Hamilton " :

" I hope, Lady Hamilton, you are pleased with
what we have been able to do for your son."

" More than pleased, your Majesty," replied
Lady Hamilton. " I am deeply and eternally
grateful both to yourself and to the Emperor.

And if my son ever comes into his inheritance as an English gentleman there will be one Englishman who can never speak or think of your Majesty except with the liveliest gratitude."

" I and the Emperor were peculiarly gratified at the refusal of your son and Captain St. Arnaud to accept of their parole when offered it by the King of Prussia. And the marvellous escape they made gave us as much pleasure as it did chagrin to the King of Prussia. These incidents of personal daring are of great value in keeping up the spirits of men engaged in defending us against the perpetual assaults of Prussia."

Lady Hamilton bowed deeply, and passed on.

It was Gavin's turn next, and to him Maria Theresa made one of those tactful speeches which, coming from a sincere heart, never failed to win the hearts of others.

" I have had great pleasure in meeting Lady Hamilton. You are fortunate in having such a mother."

Gavin's eyes shone so brightly and his face coloured so deeply with pleasure that he was on the point of forgetting what little court etiquette he had learned by dropping on his knee and seizing the Empress Queen's hands and kissing them vio-

lently. Some remnant of self-control saved him,
but his air and manner indicated so much joy,
. pride, and gratitude that a smile went around the
whole circle of onlookers, not even excepting
the Empress Queen and Emperor.

Lady Hamilton had thought that years of poverty and obscurity would give her a dislike for the
brilliant scenes of a court levee. On the contrary,
she found herself taking pleasure in a society for
which her birth and education originally fitted her.
She was haunted, however, by a horror of Sir
Gavin Hamilton's appearance. Great as had been
his offences toward her, he was still enough of an
object of interest to her to make her dread a possible meeting with him. She once had loved him
well, and however deep the resentment she felt
toward him, she could never regard him as an object of indifference. Gavin, manlike, could not
understand this. He did not seek the places where
he would find his father, but he certainly did not
avoid him. As he had never known affection for
his father, he could well be indifferent to meeting
him.

But to Lady Hamilton's intense relief, Sir Gavin did not appear at the levee that evening. This
was not from want of courage, but Sir Gavin

realized that he would be at a hopeless disadvantage. The sympathies of the court and society were with his wife and son, and, besides, he felt perfectly certain that no place or person would restrain Gavin if Sir Gavin failed in respect to Lady Hamilton; so Sir Gavin wisely went somewhere else for the early part of the evening.

Eleven o'clock was the hour when the specially favoured were to assemble at the Chancellor's splendid house. It had just struck the hour when Gavin escorted his mother up the broad marble stairs of the Chancellery and into a cosy little drawing-room, where a choice company were assembled. St. Arnaud was there before them, and in a moment more Prince Kaunitz came in, with profuse apologies for being later than his guests.

"But I really believe," he complained, "that the Empress Queen can work twenty-four hours in the day, and she wishes me to do the same. Will you believe it, in the middle of the levee she sent me word that I must look over a batch of dispatches, awaiting me in her closet, and I actually fell asleep over them, as I had been at work since six this morning. After the levee her Majesty came into the closet and shook me with her own hand until I waked. And, confidentially,

I may say I did not open my eyes as soon as I
might. Then she said in the briskest tone you
can imagine: 'Come, let us to work. We must
earn our bread.' 'Thank you, madam,' I replied,
'I cannot speak for your Majesty, but I know the
Emperor and myself have earned at least a month's
bread by the work we have done this day.'
'Well,' said her Majesty, 'I have spent more
hours than either of you in state affairs to-day,
and I have likewise given, as I always do, all the
attention necessary to the education and training
of my ten children.' 'The good God has spared
me the ten children, madam, but I believe if your
Majesty had twenty children to look after, you
would still do more work than the Emperor and
myself—and we are two of the most persistently
industrious men living.' This made her Majesty
laugh, and she said: 'Poor, good Kaunitz, go
home. I have sent the Emperor to bed, and I
alone will work at these dispatches.' I would have
stayed at that, but she sent me away after a little.
So here I am, late, but glad to get here on any
terms."

The great Chancellor was a charming host, and
when they gathered around the supper-table, a
small company of the brightest wits in Vienna,

he infected every one present with his own gayety and charm. He distinguished Lady Hamilton by his attentions, and it was a small but cherished triumph for Gavin, who counted that among the happiest evenings of his life.

Supper was not over nor the guests ready to depart until some time after midnight. Others had come in, and the party grew merrier as the hours flew by. As the final move was made to go, Prince Kaunitz stood up, with a glass of champagne in his hand, and said:

" Before parting, pledge with me the health of a lady who has only lately come to adorn Vienna, but who, we hope, will long remain with us."

The Prince fixed his smiling glance upon Lady Hamilton, who sat opposite to him. She rose, too, but the smile froze on her lips and she turned deadly pale at the noiseless entrance of a person by a door directly facing her and behind Prince Kaunitz. The Chancellor, not hearing the new arrival, continued with much grace: " The lady whose health I propose is Lady Gavin Hamilton."

Lady Hamilton's sudden pallor and agitation had not escaped notice, and a slight movement on the part of the newcomer had attracted every eye to him. The Chancellor, still unhearing, happened

to glance into a tall mirror over the fireplace, opposite him, and in it he saw Sir Gavin Hamilton,
standing perfectly cool and composed, his hand on
his dress sword, and looking Lady Hamilton full
in the eye. She, blanched and trembling, yet un-
dauntedly returned his gaze as she stood. The
only change of attitude she made was to lay her
hand lightly upon the shoulder of Gavin, who sat
next her. But the action was eloquent. It was
as if she said, " Here is my charge and my pro-
tector in one."

Gavin's face had turned scarlet as his mother's
grew white. He sat quite motionless, for once not
knowing what to say or do. Many times he had
wondered what he should do when his mother and
father met, as they were likely to do at any moment after Lady Hamilton's arrival in Vienna,
and he had never yet hit upon any course of
action. But he had vauntingly said to himself,
" When the time comes I shall do the right thing."
The time had come, and he sat silent and disconcerted and feeling nothing but a furious anger and
helplessness.

Lady Hamilton continued to look Sir Gavin
calmly in the eye, and the pause grew momen-
tous. A clock ticking in the room seemed a loud

noise, so utter was the stillness. Seconds passed, which seemed minutes, and as Lady Hamilton's glance remained fixed on Sir Gavin, they seemed to change places. She grew courageous, and the crimson returned to her face; while the fresh colour left his cheeks, and he, this man of iron composure, grew tremulous. The Chancellor, who watched it all, and who enjoyed it from the bottom of his heart—for Kaunitz had an elfish spirit which made him delight in awkward *contretemps* for others—suddenly spoke in a very cool, soft voice: "Give Sir Gavin Hamilton a glass," he said to a servant. "He will join us, no doubt, in our homage to Lady Hamilton."

All there fully expected to see Sir Gavin touch his sword as he replied to Prince Kaunitz. So, indeed, he wished to do; but Lady Hamilton's steady glance held him as if by mesmeric power. Mechanically and against his own volition he raised the glass handed him by the servant to his lips and drank as the others did. Then, quickly recovering himself, he threw the costly glass on the floor, where it crashed into a hundred pieces, and, turning his back, walked quickly out.

Whatever Lady Hamilton felt, she had managed to retain her self-possession perfectly. Not so

Gavin. He felt dazed and disconcerted, and but for St. Arnaud's tactful manner of getting him out of the room would have showed the confusion which reigned in his soul. Prince Kaunitz himself put Lady Hamilton into the carriage. Gavin entered after her, and St. Arnaud, saying he wished a breath of air before going to bed, followed on foot.

Once alone in the carriage with his mother, Gavin clasped her in his arms, saying, " How proud I was of you! And how superior did you appear to the wretch—"

" Hush," replied Lady Hamilton in a strained voice; and suddenly bursting into tears, she cried: " He was not always like this. I cannot, cannot think that he was always bad. He was a gallant man and a gentleman when I married him."

Gavin remained silent, amazed and confounded at this revelation of a woman's secret tenderness, which could survive twenty years of neglect, persecution, and unspeakable humiliation.

CHAPTER VIII

THE next morning, before nine o'clock, a messenger came from the Empress Queen to St. Arnaud, commanding his immediate presence at the imperial palace.

St. Arnaud reappeared at dusk in the evening. Gavin was sitting by the window, listening with amusement to the stories Lady Hamilton was telling, in her soft, pleasant voice, to the two little girls, Freda and Gretchen.

"Make ready," said St. Arnaud to Gavin as he came in, "to start for Breslau with me to-morrow, at midnight, with a flag of truce to the King of Prussia. I was sent for by the Empress Queen for that purpose. All is settled. I was allowed to choose a brother officer to accompany me, and I chose you."

"A thousand, thousand thanks," cried Gavin, who realized the advantages of being sent upon such an expedition.

"I warn you, though," continued St. Arnaud,

warming himself by the fire, as the little girls
lighted the candles and Lady Hamilton and Gavin
hung breathless upon his words, " our mission will
fail. The King of Prussia has never been celebrated for his kindness to the unfortunate, whether
prisoners, whom he generally browbeats, no matter
how humble or how exalted their station, or officers
of his own who do not prove always equal to victory. The Prince of Bevern, who was taken prisoner while reconnoitring near Breslau last October, wishes a letter conveyed to the King of Prussia, in winter quarters at Breslau. The Prince,
you must know, being an ally of Frederick's, fully
expected steps to be taken at once to secure his release on parole. But so far the King of Prussia
has not written him a line, or shown the slightest
interest in the fate of one of his best friends and
generals. The poor Prince, tired with waiting,
declares there must be some misapprehension on
the King's part, and solicited the Empress Queen
to allow him to send a letter to the King
at Breslau. She at once agreed, for she is
as kind to prisoners and considerate of their
feelings as Frederick is to the contrary. She,
therefore, from the goodness of her heart, consented to transmit the letter, but, as it often is, there
167

is sound political wisdom as well as generosity in
her action; because, if Frederick wishes to be-
friend his ally, the Prince can be exchanged for
a large number of Austrian prisoners, and if his
neglect is intentional, it will place Maria Theresa's conduct in shining contrast to her great
enemy's. The Emperor and Prince Kaunitz saw
this when they agreed to her generous proposal.
The Prince intimated a wish that I might be the
officer sent—I was able to show him a trifling
kindness once some years ago—and the Empress
Queen assented with the utmost alacrity. Great
and magnanimous as she is, she is woman enough
to be willing to let the King of Prussia see us,
his two prisoners, free and in good case. All arrangements are made. I have letters and money
and horses, and we start on the stroke of midnight
to-morrow. We shall probably be gone two weeks,
but if we are caught by the spring floods, we shall
be detained until they subside, for the Empress
Queen and the King of Prussia between them have
scarcely left a bridge standing in Silesia."

Gavin was overjoyed at the prospect of an expedition of so much interest; and his mother
showed her sympathy with him by at once beginning to talk over preparations. Gavin ran down-

stairs to Madame Ziska, who was just arranging the lamp and fire, and placing Kalenga with a book for the evening, before going to the opera.

" I am charmed," she cried, " although we shall be lonely without you and Captain St. Arnaud. But you will have so much to tell us when you get back! We shall be glad to take care of Lady Hamilton while you are away. Luckily, I do not dance to-morrow night, so we can spend the evening together."

The Empress Queen, with her usual liberality, which sometimes exceeded her means, having provided them with a considerable sum of money, next day they made comfortable arrangements for the journey. Prince Kaunitz offered them a small but excellent travelling chaise, which, being brought to the house, Lady Hamilton and Madame Ziska proceeded to stock with comforts not likely to be found on the road. By eight o'clock their preparations were complete, and they sat down to a merry supper in Madame Ziska's apartment.

" I shall miss you both more than I can say," said Lady Hamilton, " and I shall not go to the palace or accept any invitations until you return. But that I will not mind. I shall amuse myself,

if Madame Ziska will permit, by teaching Freda
and Gretchen English, and so the weeks will pass
more quickly."

" I shall be only too grateful," quickly replied
Madame Ziska, who saw the advantage of her two
young daughters having the training of a woman
so highly educated and well bred as Lady Hamilton.

" And pray," she continued, laughing, as they
drew up to the table, " to make my most respectful
compliments to the King of Prussia, and to tell him
that his snuff-box was treated with the highest respect wherever I showed it, and often got me ac-
commodations at inns and post-houses when it
would have been otherwise impossible. Likewise
say to him, that I think my dancing has improved
—the Emperor has been pleased to say that the
ballerina of the Queen of the Naiads is the best
thing yet done at the opera."

St. Arnaud and Gavin faithfully promised all.

The evening sped rapidly away, all, even Kalenga, being in the highest spirits. When the
clock struck twelve, and the chaise was at the door,
Kalenga, raising himself in his wheeled chair,
proposed the health of the two departing ones,
which was drank with enthusiasm. Then fol-

lowed affectionate farewells, Gavin running back
from the door for a last embrace from his mother,
and soon they were clattering off over the frozen
roadway toward the gates of the city.

As soon as they had passed the gates, and got
into the open country beyond, St. Arnaud, who was
an experienced traveller, settled himself to sleep;
but Gavin, who had never made a journey in a
chaise before, was too excited to sleep. He com-
pared his lot then—an officer with a recognized
position as a gentleman, regular, though small pay,
his mother with him, her position recognized, a
powerful friend in St. Arnaud, and other true
friends in Madame Ziska and her husband, the
protection of a great and generous sovereign like
Maria Theresa—and the contemplation of these
things caused a wave of reverential gratitude to
overwhelm his soul. A year before he had been
a private soldier, with all the hardships of a private soldier's lot in those times. He had been
ragged and cold and hungry; his fellow-soldiers,
brave, honest fellows though they might be, were
rude and ignorant men, of coarse manners, and
rarely could any of them read or write. He recalled that he had not been really unhappy during
the time that he had trudged along, carrying a

musket—in fact, it gave him something like a shock to remember that he had begun to like the life, and felt less and less the ambition to rise to something better. Perhaps he would have risen in any event, but, surely, the finding himself alone with St. Arnaud in a freezing desert after Rosbach was the most fortunate circumstance of his whole life. These thoughts crowded upon his mind, but after a while the steady motion of the chaise made him drowsy, and he slept.

Seven days were they on the journey, although they travelled as fast as the state of the country would permit, and at noon on the seventh day they came within sight of the towers and steeples of Breslau, and met the Prussian outposts.

St. Arnaud, tying his white handkerchief to the point of his sword, got out of the chaise, as did Gavin, and advanced toward the Prussian sentinel. The officer of the guard was at once sent for, and after a very short delay they were blindfolded and driven inside the walls and fortifications.

It was a tedious drive to the quarters courteously provided for them, and both St. Arnaud and Gavin suspected that they were being driven in a roundabout manner, to confuse their sense of locality.

Arrived at their quarters, the Prussian officer, Lieutenant Bohlen, led them into a room, and exacting the usual promises from them that they would not leave the house without permission and an escort, removed the handkerchiefs from their eyes. He then left, to report their arrival at head-quarters, after ordering dinner to be sent them. The dinner was very good, and they were still at it when Lieutenant Bohlen returned.

"The King will see you to-night after he has supped, and meanwhile desires that you be made comfortable."

Gavin spent a good part of the afternoon mak-ing a toilet for the King of Prussia. He bathed and shaved, and put on clean linen from top to toe, and his handsome white uniform and var-nished boots.

"And I think," he complacently remarked to St. Arnaud, "the King will find me a different person from the great gaby he hauled out of the closet. Oh, I shall never forgive myself for not knocking him down—I could have done it so easily."

St. Arnaud, too, had made an elaborate toilet, and as he surveyed himself and Gavin, he rather wounded Gavin's self-love by saying:

" You and I are obliged to dress well. The King of Prussia is shabbier than any captain in his army—but—he is the King of Prussia, and he can afford to be shabby."

About eight o'clock in the evening, another officer, Major Count von Armfeld, appeared, and politely introducing himself as aide-de-camp to his Majesty, requested them to go with him.

It was a beautiful moonlight night as the party emerged into one of the quaintest and oldest streets of Breslau. They were near a splendid bridge across the Oder, and the moon shone brightly on the placid bosom of the river. Everywhere were the signs of military occupation. Churches had been turned into barracks, public buildings into arsenals, and nearly every house had officers billeted in it.

After crossing the bridge, they entered a handsome street, at the end of which was a large and splendid mansion. A couple of sentinels were pacing before the door.

" That is where his Majesty lives," said Von Armfeld. " It is called the King's House. It has a garden to it, in which the King takes exercise."

Von Armfeld giving the countersign, they en-

tered the mansion, and ascended a handsome staircase. The house seemed to be buzzing like a bee-
hive, all the rooms being lighted up, and officers
at work in them. At the end of a long corridor
was a small door, before which they stopped. Von
Armfeld gave four peculiar raps on the door; a
voice said, " Come "—and St. Arnaud and Gavin
found themselves in the presence of the great Frederick. He was sitting by the fire and was wrapped
in an old military cape. His face was cadav-
erous, his eyes sunken, and his whole appearance
so changed by ill health, that St. Arnaud and Gavin would have had difficulty in recognizing him.
But if they found recognition of the King difficult, the King found recognition of them impossible. He looked at them as if he had never seen
them before, and motioning them to sit, consulted
a little memorandum before him.

" Captain St. Arnaud of Major-General Loudon's corps and companion, Sublieutenant Hamilton. I knew General Loudon. I might have had
his services when he returned from Russia, but I
frankly admit I saw not the man of genius under
his unpromising exterior. At the blockade of
Prague, his patent as Major-General, sent him by
the Empress Queen, fell into the hands of some of

my hussars. I had it returned to him, and was pleased to serve so gallant an officer."

St. Arnaud bowed at these praises of his commander, and after a pause Frederick said negligently:

" Have you the Prince of Bevern's letter ? "

St. Arnaud rose, and taking the Prince of Bevern's letter from his breast, handed it to Frederick, with another bow. It was a long letter, and both St. Arnaud and Gavin watched the King closely as he read. He had a speaking face, and as he read page after page of the letter his countenance grew more sinister. St. Arnaud gave Gavin a slight glance, which said plainly: " The Prince will get no help."

After reading it over carefully, Frederick laid it down, and began to speak on the topic, apparently, the farthest off, in more ways than one, from Bevern's letter that could be imagined.

" Did you ever study astronomy, Captain St. Arnaud ? "

" Considerably, your Majesty. When I was at the College of St. Omer's in France—for I had some education before I joined the army—I was much interested in it, and spent many nights at the telescope."

"I confess, I knew very little about the science. There is a garden communicating with the one we have here, and in it is an observatory with a fine telescope. I have been troubled with sleeplessness this winter, and I have spent many hours, in consequence, studying the planets. I have found it singularly soothing. Nothing so reconciles one to the chances and changes of this life as looking through a telescope. There one sees the infinite smallness of triumphs; the utter nothingness of misfortunes."

"True, your Majesty," replied St. Arnaud, as composedly as if he had come all the way from Vienna to discuss astronomy. "Of course, the uppermost thought in every mind is whether those infinite worlds are inhabited or not."

"It is a thought too staggering to pursue very far. The first conception of space is noble and exhilarating beyond expression. But I believe that the strongest mind, fixed perpetually on the vast possibilities of the solar system, would become unbalanced. Astronomers do not become so, because they pursue the science with exactness, and do not let imagination into the matter at all. But for persons like you and me, who look at the myriads of worlds with the eye of speculation,

177

it soon ceases to be exhilarating; it becomes overwhelming, and I, for one, dare not dwell too long upon it. The night is clear. Will you go with me to the observatory ? "

" Certainly," replied St. Arnaud, without showing the faintest surprise.

Frederick rose, and as he did so he fell into a violent paroxysm of coughing. When it was over he sank into his seat, too overcome with weakness to stand. Annoyance was pictured on his face at this exhibition of illness before the officers of the Empress Queen, and also a spirit of iron determination. His soul was ever stronger than his body, and in this case he triumphed over illness and exhaustion. After a few moments he rose, and going toward the door, St. Arnaud respectfully opened it, and he passed out. He held his hat in his hand, but had omitted to take his cloak, which hung over the back of his chair. St. Arnaud had not noticed the omission, but Gavin had, and picking the cloak up, he ran after the King, saying, " Your Majesty would do well to take this; the night air is sharp."

Frederick, with the ghost of a smile, proceeded to wrap himself up in the cloak, and then said: " You may come also."

Nothing loath, Gavin followed. Crossing a large garden, they ascended the stairs of a moderately tall observatory. The effort made Frederick gasp and tremble, but his step never faltered as he climbed up. Reaching the top, he struck his flint and steel, and with St. Arnaud's assistance he lighted a large lamp, saying, " That is visible from every part of the house, and signifies I am in the observatory, and I am not to be disturbed."

The telescope was soon arranged, and the King and St. Arnaud were deep in astronomical surveys and discussions. St. Arnaud was singularly well versed in astronomy, and Frederick seemed to be fascinated by his intelligent conversation. Gavin, a mute listener, sat near by, and longed unspeakably for a glimpse through the telescope.

An hour passed, and at the end of that time, while St. Arnaud was giving his views in his clear and musical voice on certain aspects of the planet Saturn, Frederick's head sunk back in his chair, his head rested against the wall, and he slept peacefully.

Neither St. Arnaud nor Gavin could restrain a feeling of pity for him then. His face, thin and drawn, was a picture of sadness. He looked not only ill, but frightfully worn, and his sleep was the sleep of exhaustion.

St. Arnaud raised his hand as a sign to Gavin to keep perfectly still. He remembered the King's remark, that he had not slept well of late, and thought this sudden drowsiness probably a blessed relief. So, indeed, it was. Gradually, as he slept more soundly, his face lost its look of pain. Soon it was plain there was no danger of his awaking. It grew chill in the room, and Gavin, softly taking off his own cloak, laid it over Frederick's knees. The warmth appeared to soothe him still more; he sighed profoundly, settled himself more comfortably in his chair, and slept like a child.

Hours passed. No one came to disturb them, for the light shining through the window was a warning that no one must enter. The town grew still as the night advanced, and in the deep silence nothing was heard but the faint tramp of sentries and the quiet flow of the river. But after midnight this changed. The wind rose, clouds of inky blackness scurried across the face of the moon, and presently it began to rain furiously. The heavy drops battered down like thunder upon the roof of the observatory, but no sound awakened Frederick, who slumbered peacefully on.

Not so Gavin and St. Arnaud, both of whom sat up, wide-awake. There was so little chance of awaking the King that they conversed together in whispers.

"What did you see through the telescope?" asked Gavin.

"That the King has no mind to help the Prince of Bevern. I saw it as plainly as I saw the moon."

"It is strange he did not recognize us."

At which St. Arnaud made a gesture which indicated that Frederick knew them quite as well as they knew him, but for reasons known only to himself did not choose to admit it.

About two o'clock the storm increased in severity. The sound of the rushing river was distinctly heard over the wild swirl of wind and rain. Presently there was a roar of waters, and looking out of the window into the garden, forty feet below, they saw it was flooded several feet. A culvert had given way, and the swollen river poured itself into the garden.

In the house lights were moving about. The King's household had determined, in spite of his rigid prohibition, to come to the observatory after him. But it was a question how they could get

181

there, as the water was already four feet deep and rising rapidly.

Just at this moment Frederick stirred in his sleep and waked. Like a true soldier, he had his memory and all his wits about him the instant he opened his eyes. He rose at once, and hearing the noise of the storm, said:

"I must have slept many hours—more than I have slept in a week. I feel much better for it."

"Look, your Majesty," said St. Arnaud, opening the window.

Frederick looked out, and as he looked he laughed. The running about in the house was plainly visible by the moving and flashing lights.

"They are all in a panic over there. I suppose they will be sending after me in a boat. It will take time to find me."

"Pardon me, sire," said Gavin. "If your Majesty will trust yourself on my back, I can get you over safely. The water is not yet up to my waist, and the distance is short."

"Yes," cried Frederick, laughing again. "While my staff are racing about like frightened chickens in a barnyard I will walk in on them." He stooped and picked up Gavin's cloak, which lay on the floor.

"I remember your laying this over my knees, although you thought I was sleeping too soundly to know anything; but come, the water rises every moment."

He went rapidly down the stairs, followed closely by Gavin and St. Arnaud. Gavin stepped boldly into the flood, which was up to his waist, and cried to the King:

"Your Majesty must make yourself very small, for my honour is engaged to get you across without wetting you. And you must also wear my cloak over your own."

Frederick sprang up on Gavin's back with great agility, drawing his heels up under Gavin's arms. St. Arnaud covered him up well with the two cloaks, and Gavin stepped lightly forward into the flood. His young strength enabled him to withstand the flow of the waters with considerable steadiness, and it was plain he could get the King over without difficulty. About midway, however, he came to a dead stop.

"Your Majesty," he asked, "do you remember us, and that night at the country house in Silesia, and Madame Ziska?"

"Certainly I do," coolly responded Frederick, "and had you not lost your senses, it would have

183

been by no means impossible for you to have made your escape by a rush, when I broke the door in."

"So I have often thought, your Majesty, if only I had had the wit to knock your Majesty down. We declined to accept your parole, but you see we got away from Glatz just the same."

"I know it. That ridiculous old Kollnitz and his 'system.' But I have a better man there than Kollnitz. You could not do it so easily now."

"Sire, the Empress Queen gave me a sword for that escape, and both of us got promotion."

"Very naturally. Women are always taken with those showy things, which count, however, for little in the long run. Your Empress Queen is like the rest of her sex."

"Sire, I do not know if you mean that disrespectfully or not, but if you say one disparaging word about my sovereign I will drop you into the water if I am shot for it to-morrow morning."

"Then I shall certainly speak of the Empress Queen with the highest respect, and feel it, too, until I am safe on dry land. Oh, the devil! Go on!"

"With pleasure, sire, since you have so handsomely respected my wishes," replied Gavin, and a few more strides brought him to the house.

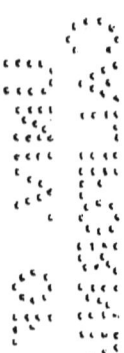

The steps were submerged, but a window on the ground floor was yet a few inches above the water. A general in epaulets and a cook with a paper cap on his head heard the sound as the King rapped loudly on the panes. The window was raised by them, and with their help Frederick stepped inside. When he threw off his outer cloak he was as dry as a bone. Gavin, who had climbed in after him, was like a river god, water streaming from every part of him. Frederick, who disliked to be questioned, said to the officer:

" Take this gentleman and provide him with dry clothes. He is Lieutenant Gavin Hamilton of the Imperialist army, as you know. His companion, Captain St. Arnaud, is still at the observatory. Let a boat be sent for Captain St. Arnaud as soon as possible."

While Frederick was speaking, he had turned to a table near by, and was writing a few words rapidly. He handed the sheet of paper to Gavin. On it was scrawled in the King's peculiar handwriting: " On the night of the first of March, 1758, Lieutenant Gavin Hamilton brought me on his back through my flooded garden at Breslau, with the water four feet deep. Midway he stopped and we conversed. The name of the Empress Queen being mentioned, Lieutenant Hamilton told me if I should speak disrespectfully of her Majesty he would drop me in the water if he were shot next morning for it. I had no thought of speaking disrespectfully of her Majesty, but if I had done so, I have no doubt Lieutenant Hamilton would have instantly carried out his threat. Frédéric."

Gavin's mouth came open in a tremendous grin as he read this, the more so when Frederick good-humouredly added:

" That ought to be good for one step in promotion at least."

CHAPTER IX

ALL through the night the storm raged. The air grew warm and murky, and thunder and lightning roared and flashed. The river, swollen by other streams, overflowed its banks, and flooded all of the old part of the town where the King's headquarters were. St. Arnaud had been brought from the observatory in a boat, and had got drenched to the bone in the process. There was no possibility at that hour, between two and three in the morning, of St. Arnaud and Gavin getting back to their own quarters. Supplied with dry clothes by the officers of the King's military family, and given a room with a bed and a sofa in it, they threw themselves down, still dressed, to sleep. Gavin, with the readiness of a child to go to sleep, dropped into a deep slumber within two minutes. St. Arnaud, much fatigued, yet found himself kept awake by the commotion of the storm. Great peals of deafening thunder shook the house; the wind, blowing frightfully hard, rattled the windows until it sounded like a continuous discharge of musketry. The surging of the waters could be heard only at intervals, while torrents of rain descended. St. Arnaud, weary, but quite unable to sleep, rose, and went to the window. The blackness of darkness encompassed everything except for the lightning flashes, which zigzagged across the inky sky, showing the whole dreadful scene. The streets were altogether submerged, and both sentry boxes had floated away. Trees were twisted off and sent scurrying along the raging waters; some bodies of drowned animals floated by.

In the gleam of the lightning St. Arnaud saw that all the houses in the neighbourhood were lighted up and the people astir. In the house in which he was no one slept except Gavin. St. Arnaud heard officers moving about, prepared, in case of a catastrophe, which was far from improbable.

As the wild sky turned from black to a pallid gray, without any abatement of the storm, St. Arnaud saw all the destruction it had wrought. Opposite him was a house with far-projecting eaves. The wind, which had lulled somewhat, suddenly rose to a gust, and the roof went skyward with a crash of breaking timbers. A cry from invisible sources rent the air, as, at a window, in the roofless house, appeared a man, half dressed. The house shook and tottered, the walls seeming about to fall in. The man, a young fellow, evidently a workman, coolly prepared to spring into the water. He leaped none too soon. The walls, weakened by the floods and the tearing away of the roof, cracked inward as he struck the water. He was evidently no swimmer, but with great self-possession floated flat on his back. A dozen persons appeared at the neighbouring windows, ready to assist him; but, carried by the flood, he was floating straight for a little balcony on which the window of St. Arnaud's room opened. St. Arnaud stepped out promptly, to catch him as he passed; but to his surprise looked up, and Gavin was beside him.

"That infernal racket waked me at last," he said.

Both of them sat astride the balustrade in order to catch the man still floating straight toward them. He reached Gavin first, who, leaning forward, with his long, muscular arms outstretched, caught him firmly, and proceeded to drag him on to the balcony by main force. In some way, however, Gavin lost his balance, and if St. Arnaud had not

come to the rescue would have gone over himself.
As it was, he could do little toward helping St.
Arnaud to drag the workman on to the balcony;
and as soon as it was accomplished he limped inside the open window. Half a dozen officers,
among them the King's surgeon, were then in the
room to assist the workman, who had suffered nothing worse than a wetting, and to ask if there were
any persons in the house when it collapsed. There
were none, and a servant was directed to take the
man below and give him some dry clothes. While
this was going on no one noticed Gavin, who sat on
a chair, nursing his leg. When they turned to
him, however, he was slipping off his chair, and the
next instant he lay in a heap on the floor, in a dead
faint.

The King's surgeon was down on his knees in
a moment, trying to bring Gavin to, while his
clothes were unloosed by St. Arnaud. In a few
minutes he recovered, only to groan with pain.
His leg was badly wrenched, and when the surgeon examined it, he horrified both Gavin and St.
Arnaud by saying:

"You have a bad sprain, and you will not be
able to move to-day or to-morrow, or for a good
many days to come."

And too true it proved.

With daylight came an abatement of the storm, but an increase of the flood. There had been many casualties, and as long as the flood lasted there was great danger. The King, who had not slept since he left the observatory, was active in taking measures of safety for the soldiers and citizens; but he did not forget to have Gavin and St. Arnaud made comfortable. He expressed much sympathy for Gavin's misfortune, inquired how they were lodged, ordered two communicating rooms to be given to them, and desired them to ask for anything they wished.

Their position, however, was highly uncomfortable. Gavin proved the worst of patients from the beginning. He was fretful and irritable, impatient of pain, and made himself much worse by his wilfulness and childishness. St. Arnaud, whom he adored, was the chief victim of his wrath. Nothing could exceed St. Arnaud's kindness and unflagging attention, but it was helpless to soothe Gavin. When St. Arnaud was present, everything he said and did was wrong. When he was absent for a few moments, he was met with a storm of reproaches on his return. He bore it all with smiling patience; but when once he could not refrain

191

from laughing, Gavin threw himself about so, in his agony of impatience, that even St. Arnaud was a little frightened.

On the evening of the day of the accident, the King sent word that he would come, after he had supped, and see Lieutenant Hamilton. St. Arnaud proceeded to make him ready. He lay on a sofa, his unlucky leg on a chair. He growled and grumbled when St. Arnaud, with the tenderness and dexterity of a woman, made him presentable for the King. As St. Arnaud brushed Gavin's dark hair, which he had let grow in ringlets since he had become an officer, Gavin snapped out:

" I did not curry my horse so hard when I was a private soldier."

" Perhaps not," replied St. Arnaud coolly; "but you must remember I am not used to currying horses—I have had no instruction in that line."

Gavin remained silent, but only slightly ashamed.

St. Arnaud had a real fear that Gavin would not behave himself properly on the occasion of the King's visit; but he had not altogether given the complete rein to folly.

About eight o'clock, the King, entirely unat-

tended, entered. Frederick of Prussia had a pas-
sion for men of *esprit,* and at this period of his
career, having lost much of his taste for the other
amusements of life, he grew more fond of the
society of brilliant and polished men than ever before. Especially was this true concerning Frenchmen, who had for him a peculiar charm; and St.
Arnaud, on the two occasions they had met, had
afforded him extreme entertainment. On St. Arnaud's part, he perfectly understood how far he
stood in the King's good graces. A knowledge of
courts had given him a just appreciation of this
sort of favour from princes; he did not delude himself with the idea that it meant a solid regard, and
he despised the understandings of those who take
the chance liking of monarchs for more than what
it is. He maintained, therefore, with Frederick
an attitude of easy, but respectful independence,
which gave their intercourse enough of equality
to be agreeable. As for Gavin, Frederick only remembered him as a spirited but rather awkward
boy; however, Gavin's threat to throw him into
the water if he spoke disrespectfully of the Empress Queen had diverted him extremely, and to
divert the King of Prussia once was a guarantee of
being expected to do it again.

Gavin, who was lying on the sofa with his leg on a chair, endeavoured to rise, as St. Arnaud did, when the King entered; but Frederick good-naturedly ordered him to keep still.

"I shall not take advantage of your helplessness to speak disrespectfully of the Empress Queen," he said, laughing; and motioning St. Arnaud to be seated, drew a chair up to the fire.

"The fact is," he continued, with a slight laugh, as musical as his delightful voice, "I never speak disrespectfully of her Majesty. It has been my misfortune to be much disliked by two ladies—the Czarina of Russia and the Empress Queen—and, consequently, I have led a bad life of it for several years. These two ladies, between them, and with the assistance of the Dauphiness of France, have leagued against me populations amounting to a hundred millions of souls. There are not five millions of Prussians; but we have tried to give a good account of ourselves."

"And your Majesty has certainly done so," replied St. Arnaud. "Luckily for us, your Majesty does not command everywhere."

"No; and I have Winterfeld no longer."

St. Arnaud had perfect control of his countenance, and it was design, and not inadvertence which made him, at the mention of Winterfeld, fix his clear eyes upon Frederick's, equally clear, and piercing in their power of expression. He remembered that General Winterfeld, who had been called the King's only friend, had lost his life at the beginning of the Prince of Bevern's unfortunate campaign, and it had been said that Frederick held Bevern's faulty arrangements partly accountable for Winterfeld's death.

After a pause, St. Arnaud spoke:

" General Winterfeld was under the command of the Prince of Bevern, to whom I am indebted for the opportunity of seeing your Majesty at this time."

A smile, faint but full of meaning and not altogether pleasant, appeared in the corners of Frederick's mouth and shone in his eyes.

" Yes," he said, tapping his breast. " I have Bevern's letter here. I have read it attentively. Be sure you tell him that."

" And permit me, sire, to say, that I apprehend I shall have no other reply to take the Prince of Bevern when I return."

" You are a good diplomatist, Captain St. Arnaud. You know my meaning, without plaguing me with questions."

" Thanks, sire; and as far as my errand goes I might leave to-morrow morning. But this young gentleman will not be able to move for a week at least, so the surgeon says."

" And there is not a bridge standing within fifty miles, I hear. So make yourself satisfied, and exchange winter quarters at Breslau for winter quarters at Vienna for a little while. You will not find it gay. Last month, my sister, the Princess Amelia, was here, and there were some balls and concerts; but as the time for taking the field approaches there is work to be done. I have been wretchedly ill, and do not think I shall be well until spring opens, and I again sleep in a tent with the flap open."

" Beating us evidently does not agree with your Majesty's health."

" Ah, well! This year—who knows? But, as you are a well-informed man, can you tell me of any campaign of ancient or modern times in which there have been such vast vicissitudes as in the last eight months? "

" Indeed, I cannot, your Majesty. The French and Austrians have alternated a *Te Deum* with a *De profundis* ever since this year's leaves appeared on the trees."

"So have I. Those two ladies I spoke of in
Austria and Russia have given me no peace at all,
nor do they seem likely to. I hear the Empress
Queen has horsed her artillery from the imperial
stables. We are quits, for I have melted up mountains of useless silver knick-knacks at my unused
palaces for money for my pay chest. You see, I
am frank—the wiseacres say I am too free in my
talk—but I take it, that the world notes my determination to maintain my kingdom the better
only for seeing how ready I am to sacrifice for
my army the baubles which most kings cherish far
beyond their value."

"True, sire, her Majesty made no secret of it
when she ordered the doors of the imperial stables
to be thrown wide, and Field-Marshal Daun to
take the best of all he saw."

During this talk Gavin had listened with all
his ears. The reflection came to him with great
force, "How much more is there in personality than
in words! Everything said by this great man,
no matter how much it resembles the language of
other men, has a deeper significance. His beautiful and eloquent eyes and his strangely musical
voice make even his most ordinary conversation
memorable." And for once Gavin was willing to

remain silent and a listener; so, too, was St. Arnaud; but Frederick was an admirable talker in two senses—he listened as gracefully as he talked, and his pleasure in being entertained was as strong as his pleasure in entertaining. He led St. Arnaud to speak of the French court. St. Arnaud, who had infinite tact, managed to describe it without touching on the ugly side of it—the scandals, the corruption, the weakness of the King, and the ascendancy of Madame de Pompadour. He did not once mention the favourite's name; but when a pause in the conversation came, Frederick said suddenly:

" And how about Madame de Pompadour ? "

" I thought, sire," responded St. Arnaud, " that you did not know of her existence. At least, M. Voltaire says when he gave you Madame de Pompadour's regards, you said, ' I don't know her.' "

Frederick looked gravely into St. Arnaud's eyes, and then they both burst out laughing, and Frederick said:

" You should have seen M. Voltaire's face before and after I made my remark. Harlequin in the show did not change so rapidly. I think that lady does not like me, either; and as for your Dauphiness—well, I am truly unfortunate in be-

ing so unpopular with the fair sex. I have done
nothing to deserve it. Had they but allowed me
to remain in peace! For peace is my dream, let
me tell you. A man must have his dreams; who
should know that better than I, whose early life
was all spent in dreams? Even now I am fighting
to conquer a peace."

"So say all great captains, sire."

"True; but most great captains have ulterior
views. I have already all I want in this life—the
throne of Prussia—if only those ladies I spoke of
would let me enjoy it in quietness."

"And the Empress Queen bewails daily that
she, too, must ever be at war. If only she and the
Emperor could have a little time to enjoy their
heritage! The Empress Queen takes great interest in guns both great and small. Prince Leuch-
tenberg, who is the head of our artillery, often
comes to the palace with his books and portfolios
of drawings, and her Majesty says, ' Such beautiful guns are too good to be used in killing the
poor soldiers of the King of Prussia.' "

"But they are probably not too good to be used
in killing the King of Prussia. Eh?"

"I do not think, sire, that her Majesty counts
you among her favourites, or contemplates leaving

you any part of her private fortune, or even money to buy a mourning ring."

" She hates me like the devil. However, speaking of those guns, the Austrian artillery is as good as any in the world, my own not excepted. You did not invent the iron rammers and ramrods, but as soon as the Prince of Dessau contrived them you adopted them. Men have never ceased to labour diligently at the task of inventing implements with which to destroy men."

" And never will, sire."

" Let us be thankful that a part of their energy is put into efforts to save life. I have cause to be grateful for that, because but for the new discovery of the Jesuits' bark, I would have died of fever this winter. Even the Empress Queen would have pitied me if she had seen me in my paroxysms of burning fever and shivering cold. The Jesuits' bark, though, has helped me."

The conversation continued for hours. St. Arnaud seemed to exercise a charmed spell over Frederick, and when he laughingly owned up to a weakness for making verses, Frederick cried out with delight:

" Now have I found a man who can both fight and write. Nature had not made up her mind whether I should be a soldier or a poet or a musician when she thrust me into this world. Fate decided the question for her, but Nature will still be heard. I have made bushels of verses this last autumn, in spite of Rosbach and Leuthen. And my flute is always in my pocket, though not often at my mouth."

Gavin could remain silent no longer. He cried out:

" And, your Majesty, St. Arnaud still plays the harpsichord. Don't you remember the night you took us prisoners how beautifully he played and sang, too ? "

Frederick, who was in high good humour, laughed extremely at this, exchanging significant glances with St. Arnaud, who said:

" Pray, pardon him, sire. He has not much experience with sovereigns."

" That's true," responded Gavin; " but then, your Majesty, when one has had a man's hand on his coat collar, and has been dragged through broken glass, as I was by you, it makes one feel well acquainted with that man, even if he be a king."

An aide-de-camp, walking up and down the corridor outside the door, stopped another young officer, going in an opposite direction, whispering:

"Do you hear the King laughing in there with those two French officers? Did ever you hear him so free and merry with *us*?"

"Never."

"And did ever you hear him praise any of his own generals as he is always praising the French and Austrian generals?"

"Yes; he praised Winterfeld after he was dead."

"They have brought a letter from the Prince of Bevern, about his exchange. Do you think the King will lift his finger for Bevern?"

"As well expect water to run up hill. This King of ours is rightly called Great, but he has ever regarded misfortune as a crime. So, therefore, let us always be lucky, and we shall be rewarded."

The officer passed on, laughing. Just then St. Arnaud, opening the door of their room, respectfully ushered the King out, who was saying:

"Remember, the first clear night we go to the observatory together." The young aide, standing rigidly at attention, saluted the King, who passed on without seeing him.

Several days went by, that seemed a nightmare for Gavin, and a strange but not unpleasant dream to St. Arnaud. Gavin's injury, which was really trifling, was aggravated by his impatience. He persisted in trying to walk about his room, in spite of the surgeon's prohibition, and at the end of the week was but little better off than he had been at the beginning. St. Arnaud had his hands full in trying to take care of him, and every evening he spent with the King. Frederick, to ensure freedom from disturbance, would go to St. Arnaud's room. A harpsichord had been placed there, and often the sound of the harpsichord and flute would float out. There had been no visits for several nights to the observatory, as the wind and rain storms had been succeeded by heavy snows. St. Arnaud had completely fascinated Frederick, who was always singularly susceptible to the charm of conversation. It was impossible for any one to resist Frederick's own powers to please when he exerted himself, and St. Arnaud found himself falling more and more under the spell of a great and comprehensive mind, like that of the King of Prussia.

Within ten days, though, in spite of doing many things to retard his recovery, Gavin's leg

203

grew so much better that St. Arnaud said to the King:

"Sire, Lieutenant Hamilton is now in condition to travel, and it is our duty to return, especially out of consideration to the Prince of Bevern."

"Do not trouble yourself about Bevern. The roads are not yet in condition to travel. You will be delayed on the way. Why not remain here? Besides, to-night will be clear, and we must have another night at the telescope."

Two days passed before St. Arnaud again mentioned it to the King. Both nights had been spent in the observatory.

"Sire," he said, "I cannot any longer restrain the impatience of Lieutenant Hamilton. He is anxious to return to Vienna, and, as you know, he is very rash and inexperienced; I cannot answer for what he may say or do if he does not return at once."

"Send him to me."

Gavin, for the first time walking without a stick, went into the King's room. It was evening, and the King stood before a large fire.

"So you will not wait until the surgeons say your leg is well enough for you to travel?"

"Sire, my leg is quite well enough to travel."

"A few days more of rest would be better for it. Your friend, Captain St. Arnaud, is not so eager to leave as you are."

"Oh, your Majesty, if you talked to me as you do to St. Arnaud, I would be willing to stay, too. But I know that I am not so well worth talking to—I am not accomplished, and do not know the world and the people in it as St. Arnaud does—and, besides, I have a mother at Vienna that I had not seen for a long time until a few weeks ago."

Frederick could not forbear smiling at Gavin's *naïveté.*

"Very well," he said; "wait but two days more in patience; the moon is at the full, and I desire to study it with St. Arnaud, and by that time it will be possible for you to start."

The two days brought very great improvement to Gavin's leg. He walked about the streets, threw away his stick, packed up such belongings as he had brought with him, and announced his readiness to start at any moment. All of the second day they had expected a message from the King saying horses were at their disposal for their travelling chaise; but the only message they got from him was, that, when supper was over, he

205

would have a little concert in his own apartments, to which St. Arnaud and Gavin were asked.

"We must go. It is now too late in the day to take the road," said St. Arnaud.

Gavin, choking with rage and disappointment, said no word. St. Arnaud began to make a careful toilet, while Gavin sullenly watched him. To St. Arnaud's laughing remark, that royal invitations must always be accepted, Gavin only replied:

"The King will not know whether I am there or not."

Seeing he was in a dangerously bad humour, St. Arnaud said nothing more and left the room. As soon as he was gone Gavin sat down to the writing-table and dashed off a letter to him.

"You have just left the room for the King's apartment as I write this. That man has bewitched you. You will not leave this place for a week yet. I cannot stand it another day. I am gone. You will find me at Vienna when you arrive, which I believe will not be until the campaign actually opens, and the King is obliged to send you away. G. H."

Having written this in much haste and fury, Gavin put together his money and papers, including Frederick's memorandum concerning their conversation in the flooded garden, stowing them in his breast pocket, and, wrapping his cloak around him, walked downstairs; and watching the moment when the sentry's back was turned, slipped out of the door and into a side street.

It was already late in the evening, and the city was poorly lighted, which was favourable to his designs. He walked toward the more thinly settled quarters of the town, following the course of the river. He had no plan in his mind, and was simply yielding to a wild impulse. Not until his eye fell upon a number of boats moored near a boat-house under a bridge did a connected idea of the best mode of getting out of Breslau present itself to him. He stepped into a boat, picked up the oars, and pulled rapidly with the stream. It was quite dark, and he could only faintly discern the straggling buildings on the shore and an occasional figure flitting past in the gloom of evening. He knew nothing of the town, but felt sure that at some point the river was watched and defended. In a little while he came to that point —a bridge, near which fortifications loomed, and on which the steady tramp of a sentry's feet could be heard.

Watching until the sentry was near the end of the bridge, Gavin, with a few swift strokes, found himself in darkness under the arches. There he waited until the sentry again left the middle of the bridge, and some minutes more of hard pulling carried the boat a considerable distance down the stream. Gavin, pulling away with the greatest energy, congratulated himself on the ease with which he had got out of Breslau.

"As soon as I am quite clear of the outposts," he thought, "I will go ashore, and make straight for the nearest military post where they do not have to report at Vienna, and with my papers and my uniform I can easily get a safe-conduct through the Prussian lines. And how cheap will St. Arnaud feel when I arrive at Vienna a week ahead of him!"

Inspired with these agreeable ideas, Gavin tugged valiantly at his oars, and being heated with the exercise, took off his coat; his cloak already lay in the bottom of the boat.

Having pulled for nearly two hours, he found himself far in the open country. The moon was then rising, and by its light he saw a smooth, wide road, leading down to a landing-place. Concluding this to be a good place to disembark, he rowed ashore, put on his coat and cloak, and took the road.

He had not travelled more than two miles when he struck the highway to Breslau. He remembered various landmarks at that point, and discovered to his joy that he was quite eight miles from the city gates.

Trudging along cheerfully in the moonlight, away from Breslau, he heard behind him a clatter of hoofs. Ten or twelve troopers, with a non-commissioned officer riding at their head, were coming rapidly down the road. Involuntarily, Gavin started to conceal himself in the hedge by the roadside; but the troopers were too quick for him. One of them saw him, galloped toward him, and, seizing him by the collar, held him until the sergeant rode up.

Gavin made no effort to escape, and, in truth, was rather glad to be caught, and said promptly to the sergeant, a coarse, brutal-looking fellow:

"I am Lieutenant Hamilton, of the First Austrian Hussar Regiment. I have been to Breslau with a flag of truce with a companion, Captain St. Arnaud, of General Loudon's corps; but being impatient to return to Vienna, I quietly walked away this evening, and if you

14

can help me on my way, I shall be infinitely obliged."

"I see you wear the uniform of an Austrian officer, but what have you got to prove the remarkable tale you are telling us?" replied the sergeant gruffly.

Gavin put his hand in his breast pocket. It was quite empty.

"My papers!" he cried. "My papers and money—they are all lost! I must have left them in the boat."

"Come along with us," said the sergeant. "I have to report to my captain, who is ten miles off. I believe you are a spy, and woe befall you if my captain thinks so, too; for he had a brother strung up as a spy by you Austrians last year, and he has sworn that an Austrian officer shall swing for it." Then, to a trooper:

"Dismount, and get a horse from the farmhouse over there and follow us."

The trooper dismounted, and Gavin, obeying a signal, got into the saddle, and in another minute he was trotting briskly down the road with the party.

Gavin had scarcely heard the word spy, he was so distressed and disheartened by the loss of his money and papers. The sergeant, who rode by his side, asked him no questions, and in perfect silence they traversed the road rapidly by the light of a brilliant moon.

It was quite midnight before they halted at a little village, and, riding up to one of the chief houses, dismounted. Gavin was at once ushered into the presence of the commanding officer, Captain Dreisel, an ill-looking man, whose appearance was not improved by a dirty nightcap over a frowzy wig.

The sergeant, who was by nature a lover of sensations, coolly announced that he had captured a spy. Gavin, who had paid no attention to the man, received a sudden and terrible shock when Dreisel said, in the coolest manner in the world:

" You must disprove what this man says, or you will be hanged as a spy in twenty-four hours."

" But I am in my uniform as sublieutenant of General Loudon's hussars! I am a prisoner of war."

" So was my brother," replied Dreisel, coolly lighting a huge pipe. " Nevertheless, the Austrians hanged him. They made a thousand explanations afterward, alleged that it was an infernal mistake, and all that, and punished every-

211

body connected with the affair; but it could not
bring my brother back. And, besides, you may
have stolen that uniform. At all events, I have
three sublieutenants here, and we will settle the ;
matter for you after breakfast to-morrow morning, without troubling headquarters with it.
Meanwhile, I am going to bed. Sergeant, watch
this man;" and Dreisel sauntered into the next
room.

The sergeant, leaving a couple of soldiers on
guard, went out, and Gavin sat down on a bench
before the stove to rest, for he did not think he
could sleep. He was very hungry, and asking the
soldier who walked up and down outside the room
door if anything to eat was to be had, the man
pointed to a cupboard. Out of it Gavin got some
bread and cheese, and then, lying down on the
bench, proceeded to sum up the situation, with the
result that he considered his chances for being
hanged within the next twenty-four hours about
as certain as they well could be. But although this
was his deliberate and reasonable conclusion, it
by no means followed that he actually believed he
was going to be hanged. On the contrary, it
seemed altogether an impossibility, and the conditions surrounding him appeared to him more un-

real than the wildest dream he ever had in his
life. He pinched himself to find whether he was
awake. The last time he had eaten, before getting the bread and cheese out of the cupboard,
had been at the King's headquarters in Breslau.
He noted that the bread and cheese had no flavour
to. it; he only knew that he was eating by the
looks, not the taste. Yet, it must be something
portentous that could make him feel so strangely,
and then he recalled all the circumstances, which
led him to believe that he had fallen into the hands
of a vengeful and desperate man, and something
very like a promise had been made him that he
would be hanged within twenty-four hours; and
going over and over the whole puzzling business,
he suddenly fell asleep, his dark, boyish head resting on his arm against the wall.

At daylight he was awake in the same strange
mental state. The soldiers who guarded him were
amazed at his coolness, but it was really the in-
sensibility of a person too dazed and astounded
to think or even feel, to a great degree. He was
given a good breakfast, which he ate with appe-
tite; but he might have been eating shavings, as
far as his palate went. It annoyed him the way
the soldiers and the guard looked at him. There

was something pitying in their glance, as if they expected him to be hanged—an idea so ridiculous to Gavin that he could have laughed aloud at it. Yet it did not seem ridiculous to them, and that was both strange and disagreeable. Altogether, it was the most unpleasant morning of his life. He was left to himself all the forenoon, but soon after the captain's midday dinner he was summoned to appear in another room. Seated at the head of the table was Captain Dreisel. One look at his determined and savage countenance showed Gavin that he could not appear before a worse judge. Chance had thrown a victim in this man's way— a man looking for a victim. It was enough.

Three sublieutenants were seated also at the table, to give it something the appearance of a court martial. They were all young and beardless fellows, and what impressed Gavin as much as anything else was the distress and agitation visible upon the countenances of these young subalterns. They looked anxiously at one another, and it was plain that the work before them was not to their liking.

Gavin, after saluting, was given a chair and seated himself. Never in his life had his soul been in such a tumult as at that moment; yet never had he been outwardly more calm or more entirely in possession of his senses, which presently returned to him.

Dreisel began the examination, and Gavin told clearly and frankly all that had befallen him. But, to his consternation, he saw at every word that the three younger officers were losing confidence in him. Great as was their sympathy for him, his adventures, especially his claim of having lived at the King's headquarters for three weeks, were too unusual to be accepted without proof. And of proof he had not a scintilla.

The examination was done almost entirely by Dreisel, whose artfully contrived questions were admirably adapted to put Gavin in the worst possible light. He felt, himself, the improbable nature of some of his replies, which, though strictly truthful, yet had an appearance of extravagance. As he was plied thick and fast, answering each question eagerly, it was plain that he was not making a good impression upon the three young officers, who, he saw, hated and dreaded the outcome. He saw glances of dismay exchanged among them at some of his answers, and one of these young officers, whose countenance was particularly mild, grew paler and paler, while great drops stood out on his forehead. At last, after an hour of torture, Dreisel said to him:

"And you expect us to believe that you are not a spy?"

At the word spy Gavin involuntarily started. It was the first time the word had been uttered in the presence of the other officers. Nevertheless, he responded promptly:

"I cannot be held as a spy wearing this uniform."

"True, according to the rules of war among civilized nations. But my brother was hanged as a spy wearing the Prussian uniform."

The young officer, who had shown such unmistakable marks of distress, interposed at this:

"But the whole affair was disclaimed, sir, by the Austrian military authorities."

"Well, so may all our proceedings to-day be disclaimed by the Prussian military authorities."

Dreisel said this with a diabolical grin.

"But I am zealous in the King's cause; and if I hang a man because I think him a spy, and, moreover, has designs upon the King's life—for that is the meaning of his skulking about the King's .headquarters for three weeks—*if* he ever

was there—it ought not to go very hard with me. Let me ask each and all of you this, Do you believe all the prisoner has told us ? "

A dead silence greeted this. Dreisel called to the sergeant outside the door, and said to him when he came in:

" Take charge of the prisoner until I send for him."

Gavin rose without a word. Had words availed him, he would have poured them forth; but he saw that they were worse than useless. As he passed out, the young officer who had shown such sympathy for him half rose from his chair, and looking at Gavin with eyes of misery, seemed about to hold out his hand.

" You had better not, my friend," said Gavin, unable to keep silence any longer. " Perhaps you may be shot for shaking hands with a prisoner of war about to be hanged."

In the corridor leading to the room to which he was conveyed there was a window looking straight into the window of the court-martial room. The sentry who passed the door near which Gavin sat also passed this window in his walk up and down the corridor. Something of sympathy in the man's eye as he glanced in the room where Gavin sat, with the sergeant at his side, caused Gavin to say:

"My friend, I, too, once carried a musket before I wore a sword; therefore, I beg of you, as a comrade, to tell me what Captain Dreisel and his unhappy young officers are doing in that room."

"Lieutenant von Bulow, the soft-hearted one, is standing up speaking to Captain Dreisel," he said in a low voice.

The man walked away, and, passing the window, returned in five minutes to the open door. He again whispered:

"Lieutenant Reber is now talking very earnestly, and seems not afraid of the captain."

The third time he passed the door the sentry's face was ashy pale.

"Captain Dreisel is speaking now, and Lieutenant von Bulow has covered his face and is crying."

"Is he?" was Gavin's only remark. "Good Von Bulow. I suppose I am to be hanged. Well, I will lie down on this bench and think over things a little."

He lay out at full length on the bench, and thoughts of all sorts chased one another through his mind. He had the tenderest thoughts of his mother and of St. Arnaud and Madame Ziska

and her family, and the most acute pity for himself. "No wonder Von Bulow weeps at the
thought of an innocent young man being hanged.
I would weep for Von Bulow under the same circumstances." But he could not perceive, much to
his surprise, any sensation of fear or weakness.
He felt his pulse—it was beating with perfect
steadiness—he took up a glass of water and drank
it without the tremor of a finger, and lying calmly
down again, closed his eyes. And the soldiers
watching him saw a strange thing—his breathing
grew slower, his limbs relaxed, and he was sleeping as peacefully as an infant. Gavin himself fell
into the most delicious dream—he was walking
with his mother in the gardens at Schoenbrunn;
it was a lovely spring morning, and he carried his
hat in his hand to feel the soft, sweet breeze, and
his mother was saying to him:

"Now, dear Gavin, we shall be so happy together; there will be no more separations for us."

He was roused from this by a vigorous shaking,
and St. Arnaud's voice saying:

"Wake up! You don't seem to mind the notion of being hanged; but for my part, I could
give you ten good beatings for the misery and anxiety your folly has cost me."

CHAPTER X

GAVIN sat up, rubbed his eyes, remained silent for some minutes, while St. Arnaud berated him, winding up with:

"Two hours later, and you would have been hanged."

"I thought so, too," replied Gavin. "Dreisel, the captain, was bent on it. But how came you here?"

"By following you, of course. I left the concert early, and went to our quarters, to find you gone and your letter on the table. I gave the alarm immediately, not knowing what trouble you might get into. I suspected at once that you would try the river, as there was less chance of your being stopped, and we—Captain Bohlen and I— were after you in a boat within an hour after you took to the water. We found the boat and your papers in it—I have the papers with me—and had no difficulty in tracking you to the place where you were captured. There we had some delay. Several small bodies of men were moving about that night, and we lost some hours in finding which one had bagged you. As soon as we discovered that your friend, Captain Dreisel, was the man, we lost not a moment, for he has openly said he means to hang an Austrian officer. They were still debating when we arrived; the young sublieuten- ants showed more courage than Dreisel counted on, and threatened to refuse to obey orders if you were sentenced to be hanged. You should have seen them when Bohlen and I walked in on them. Dreisel was perfectly cool and collected; he saw that he was balked, and probably ruined for life, as Bohlen will lay the whole matter before the King. The three lieutenants nearly had hysterics from joy. Bohlen means to ask promotion for them, since they saved the Prussian army the disgrace of hanging an Austrian officer. When we asked for you, behold, you were asleep! What a fellow you are!"

Gavin sprang up, and seizing St. Arnaud around the neck, they kissed and embraced.

At that moment Gavin glanced up. Bohlen, Von Bulow, and the other two lieutenants were entering the room. They crowded around him and wrung his hand, and Von Bulow, fairly bursting into tears, embraced him. They all laughed at Von Bulow; but every man of them felt shaken by the crisis each had passed through. Turning to the soldiers, especially the sentry and the sergeant, Gavin emptied his pockets, and then with one accord all the officers went out of the house that still sheltered Dreisel.

" I breathe better," cried Von Bulow, snuffing the chill, clear air, " out of the quarters of that wretch."

" Think what we have endured since this morning," added his brother lieutenant. " We would have died where we sat rather than have acquiesced in murder; but we did not know whether our men would obey us or Dreisel."

" Never mind, gentlemen," quietly remarked Bohlen, " wait until I make my report to his Majesty. Dreisel then will rue the day he was born."

It was late in the cold March afternoon, and the village inn looked very inviting. In it they went, and spent a long evening together. Great was the jollity of all of them, except Gavin, in whom all saw the signs of a reaction. He sat silent for the most part, and his eyes, when they met those of the others, were filled with tears of grat-

itude. When they separated for the night, St.
Arnaud demanded but one room for himself and
Gavin. Alone together, Gavin broke down utterly. St. Arnaud spent the night soothing and
cheering him. And this was the man who had
gone calmly to sleep while the question of hanging
him was being debated!

Next morning, St. Arnaud announced that they
would return to Breslau, for the purpose of expressing their thanks to the King and saying farewell. As for the report of the affair, Bohlen might
be trusted to attend faithfully to that. Gavin
submitted to the delay without a word. They
reached Breslau in the afternoon, went straight
to their old quarters, and at eight o'clock—the
King's usual hour for seeing them—they were
sent for. Frederick received them with more than
his usual grace; but neither St. Arnaud nor Gavin
justly appreciated until then the true extent to
which this man should be feared. He said but
little of Dreisel; but the tones of his ringing
voice and the sombre fire that shone in his
steel-blue eyes would have made a braver man
than Dreisel tremble. Frederick did not long
dwell on the subject, which was necessarily a pain-
ful and embarrassing one for him, and soon turned

the conversation into lighter and more playful channels.

"Bohlen tells me you wish to start very early to-morrow morning," he said to St. Arnaud. " I can well believe that this young gentleman is a vast responsibility. I wish to express to you the pleasure I have had in the company of both, but especially of Captain St. Arnaud. I fear that history will say of me that I took no pleasure in anything but beating my enemy in the field. How great a mistake! I was formed for the pursuits of a peaceful but not inactive life. The reorganization of my country, the improvement of my people, a steady progress of the arts and sciences, a little recreation in the way of poetry and music, and the society of accomplished men—these would constitute my happiness. I have known but little of it. Instead I spend my summers in the saddle and my winters in planning for the summer campaign. Did but the Empress Queen command her armies in the field, as I do, she would make peace with me forever."

St. Arnaud, not caring to discuss the only terms on which Frederick would make peace, contented himself with replying:

"The world, your Majesty, is loath to credit

a man with more than one kind of excellence, and
because you are a master of the art of war, it will
always grudgingly admit what you have done or
might do in the arts of peace. I can, sire, tell you
truly, without the smallest flattery, that the hours
I have spent with your Majesty are among the
most valuable of my life; for I never failed to
learn something from you that I did not know
before."

Frederick smiled graciously; he knew St. Arnaud to be a sincere man, and that his phrases,
although courtier-like, were from an honest heart.
And when, as they shook hands cordially, St. Arnaud said:

"And have I no message for the Prince of
Bevern ?"

"None, but that I have received his letter, and
I am under great obligations to him for making
me acquainted with so agreeable a man as yourself."

Gavin then advancing, Frederick said:

"Farewell. I have not had much speech with
you, but I perceive you to be no ordinary man."

And Gavin, meaning to make a very conventional
and correct reply, said earnestly:

"Your Majesty, I have been in your company

now several times, and I never was ennuyéed for one single moment when your Majesty was speaking ! "

" Take care of him," cried the King to St. Arnaud, both of them laughing. " You have an original there, and he may either be exiled or become Prime Minister."

The return journey to Vienna was made rapidly, and on a pleasant spring night their travelling chaise rattled up to the house in the Teinfeltstrasse. They were received with open arms by Lady Hamilton and Madame Ziska and her family. St. Arnaud and Gavin had agreed to say nothing for the present about Gavin's little adventure with Captain Dreisel, and Lady Hamilton thought their journey had been one of unmixed pleasure, except for the trifling accident to Gavin's leg.

Next morning they went to the palace, and were summoned before the Empress Queen and the Emperor. St. Arnaud gave an account of their mission, together with the ill success of it for the poor Prince of Bevern. Marie Theresa listened with a scornful smile. Frederick of Prussia was not only to her the enemy of her country, but an object of the deepest personal dislike, and noth-

ing good, in her opinion, could be expected of
him.

" The conduct of the King of Prussia in this
affair does not surprise me in the least," she said;
" and so much was it expected by me, that, with
the Emperor's consent, I had already determined
upon my course toward the Prince of Bevern. He
shall be released at once and allowed to return to
his country, with no condition beyond that of not
serving against us during the present war. If the
King of Prussia has no merciful impulses toward
his officers, who, though brave, may meet with
misfortunes, I and the Emperor feel much sympathy for them; and we will do for the Prince of
Bevern what his own sovereign refuses to do.
Have you anything else of moment to tell me ? "

" Nothing, madam, except an adventure of
Lieutenant Hamilton's, which may interest you."
And St. Arnaud, with inimitable archness, told
the story of Gavin's bringing Frederick through
the flooded garden on his back, and the conversation that ensued.

The Empress Queen and the Emperor laughed
so much that Gavin, who was very red and em-
barrassed in the beginning, began to feel seriously
disconcerted. He recovered his good humour, how-

ever, when the Empress Queen desired to see
Frederick's memorandum, and after reading it
cried:

" I cannot do less than the King of Prussia expects. You shall have two steps in promotion instead of one! " At which Gavin only blushed the
more while stammering out his thanks.

When, a few moments after, St. Arnaud and
Gavin left the Empress Queen's closet, St. Arnaud
whispered:

" The release of poor Bevern is caused by two
motives—one, to benefit a brave but unfortunate
man; the other, to chagrin the King of Prussia."

The next succeeding weeks were entirely different from those which had preceded the Breslau
expedition. The spring campaign was about to
open, and court and people were absorbed in
preparations for trying the fortunes of war once
more with Frederick. St. Arnaud was busy all
day and all night with the affairs of his corps.
It had been in cantonments on the outskirts of
Vienna during the winter, and was to march the
middle of April. Gavin's duties as a subaltern
compelled him to take up his quarters with his regiment, and he occupied alone the tent that was to shel-
ter St. Arnaud and himself on the march. He applied

himself more seriously to the study of military
affairs from the point of an officer, and in this, as
in everything he had tried to study in his life, he
had much assistance from his mother. She got
him books in English and French, and helped
him in his fluent but somewhat incorrect German.
Nor were his creature comforts forgotten, although
Lady Hamilton never ceased to impress upon him
that the equipment of his mind must always come
before the considerations for his body. Nevertheless, he was well supplied with many little comforts for the campaign which had been unknown
to him before.

Every day he came to the Teinfeltstrasse house
to visit his mother, if only for a few minutes, and
to see his cherished friends, Madame Ziska and her
family. It was arranged that Lady Hamilton
should remain with her excellent friends until
Gavin could return to Vienna—if ever he returned.
Gavin, however, had perfect confidence in his own
return, for his nature was sanguine to the last degree, and it was always as surprising as it was unpleasant for things to go wrong with him. Having
escaped hanging by a very narrow margin only
gave him increased confidence in the future—a
thing very conducive to both happiness and success.

He did not again see his father, and really did not know whether Sir Gavin Hamilton was still in Vienna or not. Gavin's duties kept him so closely with his troop, that he no longer had time to frequent palaces or drawing-rooms, and it was not always easy for him to see his mother once a day. St. Arnaud was equally busy, and their thoughts and their talk were all about the coming campaign. They congratulated themselves daily upon being under General Loudon, the most adventurous of men, and the making the campaign with each other was peculiarly gratifying to both.

Daily were they expecting orders to march. Marshal Daun had begun the concentration of his army at Koniggratz the middle of March, and the light troops under General Loudon were expected to be on the move to join him by the middle of April. It was known that General Loudon was to come to Vienna to receive the Military Order of Maria Theresa—the highest military order in the Empire, and one justly earned by General Loudon—and after spending one day there, he was to accompany the very last brigade to Leutomischl, about fifty miles from Olmutz. Each day detachments were dispatched, but St. Arnaud's and Gavin's regiments were not among them. It be-

gan to be whispered abroad that their regiment
would have the honour of escorting the major-general himself.

One day, as Gavin was toiling over a muddy
road, at the head of his troop of hussars, which
had been going through the sword exercise, he
met St. Arnaud galloping along alone. He rode
up to Gavin, and called out loud enough for the
men to hear:

" By the day after to-morrow we shall be on the
march. Not half a mile behind me rides General
Loudon, and when he comes to Vienna it is for
as short a time as he can stay; and then he goes
off like a shot, hunting for Prussians."

The men exchanged glances of pleasure, and
Gavin, bringing the detachment down to a slow
trot, and talking with St. Arnaud, presently heard
the thunder of hoofs behind them. He looked
back, and there, coming along the highroad, still
muddy from the spring rains, was a small cavalry
escort, and in front rode a tall, spare, red-haired
man, whom he surmised to be the celebrated General Loudon.

Gavin, drawing his men up on the side of the
road, placed himself slightly in advance of them,
with St. Arnaud. As General Loudon came up,

he stopped and courteously saluted both officers and men, the latter raising a hearty cheer as he approached. St. Arnaud then introduced Gavin, pronouncing his name much better than Gavin could.

"Hamilton!" said General Loudon. "That is a Scotch and also an English name. How comes Lieutenant Hamilton in my command?"

"It is a long story, sir," responded Gavin; "but, like yourself, although I am of Scotch and English blood, I am a true soldier, if not a born subject, of the Empress Queen."

General Loudon then made a few remarks; but his manner, though polite, was awkward, and he had by no means the graceful self-possession of St. Arnaud or the pleasant assurance of Gavin Hamilton.

When he had ridden on St. Arnaud said to Gavin:

"Do you see how cold, how awkward, how slow he is? That man under fire becomes animated, quicker than lightning, even graceful. It has been said that he grows actually handsome in the light of battle."

"He looks like a Calvinist minister with dyspepsia," was Gavin's comment; nevertheless, he

knew very well General Loudon's reputation as
the most dashing leader of light troops in Europe.

As soon as General Loudon's arrival was known
in Vienna, it was understood that the opening of
the campaign was at hand, and there was the stir
and excitement of the actual beginning of warlike
events. The announcement was made that the Empress Queen would invest him with her great military order on the evening of the next day, and the
morning after, at sunrise, he would be on the march
for Leutomischl, with the last of the hussar regiments.

St. Arnaud and Gavin were in a fever of
preparation all that day and the next; but a duty,
not to be omitted, was their presence at the palace
in the evening to see the bestowal of this splendid
decoration on their commander. The Empress
Queen, consonant with her lofty and unquenchable
spirit, had commanded a splendid levee on the
occasion, that she might show to all the world the
courage and high hopes with which she renewed
the struggle.

Never had Gavin more admired his mother's
courage than during those last two days. Smiling,
hopeful, encouraging, she bore the terrible heart-
ache of parting, but she did not wholly hide it, even

from Gavin. For himself, he went to war as he went to a festival. He was distressed at the thought of his mother, but he was too wholly confident of returning to her to seriously grieve.

"Do this for me, mother—go with me to the palace to-night; let me have the satisfaction of showing you to all those people, and, besides, it will divert you and make you forget that I am leaving to-morrow."

"Very likely," murmured Lady Hamilton.

"And as for meeting my father, I think he must have left Vienna. No one has seen him for a month."

"Then I will go; perhaps the being with you a few hours longer may be an inducement," replied his mother in a gayer tone.

"It is every one's duty, mother, to look gay to-night; for if we meet the Prussians with downcast hearts, we are already half beaten."

"Quite true. And as I am the daughter of a soldier, and was the sister of soldiers, as well as the mother of a soldier, I shall be as brave as any. But let me tell you, Gavin, the bravest at the levee to-night will not be the men wearing their swords, but the women who with anxious hearts and trembling souls give their best beloved to their country."

Madame Ziska and Kalenga were to sit up until the return of the party from the palace, and they were to have a farewell supper together, for St. Arnaud and Gavin must be with their troops before daybreak.

Madame Ziska and little Freda assisted Lady Hamilton with her toilet—the same severely simple black satin gown she had worn before. The two women understood and mutually comforted each other, and by tacit agreement there was no mention of the impending parting until just as Lady Hamilton was ready, and stood a picture of mature and womanly grace, Madame Ziska began to weep.

"I am a fool," she cried. "They will come back—I know they will come back—but it is hard to let them go, for I, too, love them dearly."

At this Freda suddenly burst into loud weeping. The mother remained dry-eyed.

"To-morrow," she said, "there will be time enough for tears. To-night I will not show, so much as by the quiver of an eyelash, the pain and fear that are gnawing at me."

At that moment they heard Gavin and St. Arnaud in the next room. Madame Ziska quickly dried her eyes, gently pushed the weeping Freda

235

out of sight and hearing in the corridor, and appeared smiling calmly before Gavin and St. Arnaud.

"Now, this is what I wish to see," cried Gavin—"a pleasant parting, without any tears or fears. There is no doubt about it, we go to beat the Prussians; we will return with increased rank and decorations, and we will be saying among ourselves, 'How sensible it was to part gayly as we did!'"

"Quite true," said his mother, smiling, and taking St. Arnaud's arm to lead her to the coach, while Gavin lingered to say a gay farewell to Madame Ziska, and to call Freda, who remained weeping and invisible on the landing of the back stairs.

In a little while they were at the palace, where a great crowd of persons, military and civil, had assembled to do honour to the army, through General Loudon. Kaunitz was there, superbly dressed as usual, with his eagle eye fixed on the French ambassador, to make sure that he noted the loyalty and enthusiasm of all present. The young archdukes and archduchesses, from the Crown Prince, a handsome young man of seventeen, standing behind his mother's chair, down to the pretty little princesses, with their governesses, grouped in a gallery overlooking the splendid scene, were all present.

St. Arnaud and Gavin with Lady Hamilton secured a good place of observation in the grand salon, where the ceremony of bestowing the order was to take place. The Empress Queen and the Emperor sat in gilded arm-chairs upon the same daïs that they had occupied at the first royal levee Gavin had attended. The Empress Queen looked even more superb than Gavin had yet seen her. Fearful as had been the blows that had befallen her armies, she was ready again, with lion-like courage, to meet her ancient enemy. Every heart in Austria and Hungary might grow faint, but Maria Theresa knew not what fear meant. She was talking with great animation to those around her, with her fine, expressive eyes flashing, and her full, red lips wreathed in smiles. When danger was at hand, then was she most full of vivid life. The Emperor at her side showed equal cheerfulness. Occasionally, the Empress Queen would turn to him and make a smiling remark, to which he would respond in kind. At length, a hush fell upon the company; General Loudon had entered the hall. He was entirely unaccompanied, and dressed in a very splendid uniform. Immediately

237

way was made for him, and he proceeded up the aisle thus formed to the daïs. At the sight of his countenance an involuntary smile went around. His naturally rugged features looked still more homely under the embarrassment of so much notice. He ambled along with the utmost awkwardness, glanced around desperately when he reached the foot of the daïs, as if looking for a place to run away; and when the Empress Queen, with her characteristic grace, pinned the magnificent decoration on his breast, he almost fell over the royal footstool in his attempt to kneel and kiss her hand.

"Never mind," whispered St. Arnaud. "Wait until you see him leading the charge up a hill, with Prussians well posted at the top. He never falters or palters then, nor falls over anything, nor looks around to see if there is any chance of running away."

The air of hope and encouragement worn by the Empress Queen was infectious. All were under the influence of excitement, and it brought brightness to the eyes and a ringing echo to the voices of all. Never had Gavin passed a gayer evening, nor had St. Arnaud. As for Lady Hamilton, many mothers and wives and sisters were present who were no less brave than she; but if she had been asked to name one of the periods of most exquisite misery in her life, it would have been the night of that brilliant levee, when, with a head proudly erect and a smiling face, she walked through the stately splendours of a palace.

Before midnight they were home again. Madame Ziska had a delicious supper waiting for them, and Kalenga's chair was already drawn up to the table. Amid laughter and toasts and the most dazzling anticipations, on Gavin's part, of the campaign, an hour was passed. Then they heard the tramping of horses at the door, as the orderly brought them trotting down the stony street.

The children were supposed to be in bed, as Gavin and St. Arnaud were giving some last messages and little presents for them, when a door opened, and Freda and Gretchen, with the two boys, all fully dressed, walked in.

" We knew you were going away," cried Freda, trying not to cry; " so after we had been put to bed we agreed to get up and dress ourselves when you came home from the levee—and—and—"

Freda broke down, immediately followed by Gretchen and the two little boys, who considered it a mark of affection for Gavin and St. Arnaud to bawl at the top of their lungs. The two departing ones hastily kissed the children all around, and Gavin was forced to gently disentangle Freda's arms from about his neck; and wringing Kalenga's hand, they went to the door, accompanied by Lady Hamilton and Madame Ziska. Farewells, heartfelt, but silent and swift, were exchanged, and a moment after, when Gavin and St. Arnaud were clattering down the street, Gavin said in a low voice:

"The Prussians cannot make us suffer more than in parting from those we love. That last kiss of my mother's—oh, St. Arnaud, I can never, never forget it!"

CHAPTER XI

'At sunrise, on a beautiful April morning, the last detachment of General Loudon's light troops, five thousand strong, took up their march to join the army of Marshal Daun.

Every officer and man wore in his helmet a sprig of green, according to an ancient custom of the Austrian army when beginning a campaign. Vast crowds assembled at every point of vantage along the highway to applaud these favourite troops; while, afar off, the steeples, towers, and belfries of Vienna were black with people watching as this splendid body of men unwound itself, like a great serpent, and turned its head toward the enemy.

Gavin felt triumphantly happy as his troop, well horsed and clad, fell in line. They were mostly new recruits, with a sprinkling of seasoned soldiers, but they had had several months of breaking in at the cantonments, and being originally of stout fibre—honest peasantry, used to an outdoor life of toil—they were already fair soldiers. If every one of them did not burn with enthusiasm, as Gavin did, to distinguish himself, they had a fine and noble *esprit de corps,* which rendered it certain that every man would do his duty to his sovereign and his country.

St. Arnaud, as captain, had more liberty in his movements on the march than Gavin; but Gavin, riding along contentedly at the head of his troop, was well entertained by his own thoughts.

"If I expect promotion," he argued to himself, "I ought to show by the condition of the men under me how I could manage a larger body. Now, having been a private soldier myself, I know exactly what these fellows will do and will not do. They will not, at first, know how to make themselves comfortable; but I, who went through two campaigns, know a thing or two about that. Then, when a man is ill, if he is a brave fellow, he will make out that he is well, and won't go to the hospital; but I will look sharp after him and see that he does. The faint-hearted ones will imagine they are ill every time things look a little blue. Aha! I shall catch those fellows. I will have my men so that St. Arnaud will say to the major: 'Do you notice Lieutenant Hamilton's troop? Always ninety-nine per cent. of them fit for duty.' Then

242

the major, reporting to the lieutenant-colonel, will
say: 'Do you observe Lieutenant Hamilton's excellent report?' And the lieutenant-colonel, talking with the colonel, will say: 'Lieutenant Hamilton's troop is the best in St. Arnaud's command,
and St. Arnaud's command is the best in the regiment.' And the colonel, one day, as we file past,
will say to General Loudon: 'Will your Excellency
notice Captain St. Arnaud's command, how well
it looks and marches?' And General Loudon will
reply: 'True; and Lieutenant Hamilton's troop is
the best of them.' And so, when promotions are
going, it will be said: 'St. Arnaud and that young
Hamilton must not be left out.' Oh, what a stroke
of good fortune it was that I got lost in the snow
in Silesia!"

When they halted for the night, Gavin made
good all he had said concerning his knowledge of
how to make his men comfortable. His troopers,
seeing this intimate knowledge of their wants, and
that they were attended to before their young lieutenant looked after his own comfort, conceived an
instant respect for him. After he had seen that
both men and horses were provided for, Gavin has-
tened to the tent to be shared in common by St.
Arnaud and himself. St. Arnaud had been equally

zealous in the performance of his duty, and it was more onerous than Gavin's. But presently he arrived; their servant had provided them with a good supper, and they spent their first evening of campaigning with the greatest merriment.

Those days of marching toward Marshal Daun were to Gavin very happy. He loved a soldier's life, and when he had bright spring weather and mild April nights, with the comforts of an officer on the march, he had nothing else to ask for in life except promotion.

They reached the neighbourhood of Leutomischl within a few days, and found an army of fifty thousand men assembled, mostly raw recruits, with the remnants of the men who had made the disastrous autumn campaign. Forty miles off lay Frederick of Prussia, with forty thousand men, besieging Olmutz. If he succeeded in capturing this strongly fortified place the road to Vienna would be open. But it was an undertaking difficult for even the stupendous military genius of Frederick. The town was naturally protected by the numerous branches of the Morawa River, and these sluices, generally kept dammed, could easily be flooded and oppose difficult obstacles to overcome. In addition to this, all of the Prussian supplies—food, ammunition, and money—had to be transported by wagons from Neisse, a hundred and twenty miles off, while the last eighty miles from Troppau were extremely dangerous, and required a protecting force of more than ten thousand men for each of the monthly convoys of from three to four thousand four-horse wagons.

Marshal Daun was proverbial for his slowness and caution, and it was often a source of congratulation to Gavin and St. Arnaud that they were under General Loudon, who was in a state of perpetual activity. There were continual scouting parties almost to the gates of Olmutz, and constant communication with the town and garrison. Both were determined to resist, and being well provided with food and ammunition, there was no thought of surrender. Frederick, who is thought to have shown less ability in sieges than in battles, had allowed his engineers to begin their first parallel too far away from the lines, and the first bombardment, terrific in point of noise, and costing vast amounts of the gunpowder so precious to the Prussians, did not the smallest harm.

The month of May opened, and although Frederick pursued the siege with vigour, Marshal Daun still lay among the hills and mountains, moving a little off from Leutomischl, but still keeping about forty miles from Olmutz. He knew, however, that all was going well for the Austrians and ill for the Prussians at Olmutz. The Pandours, light-armed Hungarian infantry, that in marching could equal the cavalry, infested the neighbourhood of the town and fortress in small parties, and even singly, while Loudon's corps, chiefly light cavalry, but with four regiments of grenadiers, made it dangerous to all small bodies of Prussian troops who ventured away from their lines. Loudon's comprehensive and piercing eye did not fail to see the qualifications of all his officers, even the subalterns, whom he knew through the reports he exacted of their superiors, and he soon came to realize that in Captain St. Arnaud he had a man after his own heart. And riding one day with the colonel of St. Arnaud's regiment, the general said:

"Is not that young Sublieutenant Hamilton, who is always with Captain St. Arnaud, a capable officer?"

"Very, sir; his activity and enterprise, as well as Captain St. Arnaud's, were shown by their escape from Glatz. As you probably know, Hamilton is of good English and Scotch blood, but, owing to some family troubles, his youth was spent in poverty and obscurity, and he served some time in the French army as a private soldier. The Empress Queen herself gave him his commission, and the young man seems burning to distinguish himself."

General Loudon, himself a Scotchman, was not less interested in Gavin from knowing his nationality.

May passed into June, and June waned; still Marshal Daun gave no sign of interrupting the siege of Olmutz. He had merely taken up a position a few miles nearer, where he patiently waited for the hour of action. The officers and men of Loudon's corps were envied by the rest of the army, as they alone were actively employed.

One night, after a week of very active scouting, St. Arnaud and Gavin were sitting in their tent, when a message from General Loudon came for St. Arnaud. He at once left, and it was an hour before he returned. When he entered, his gleaming eyes and smiling face showed that he had something pleasant to tell.

" Good news! great news! " he said, sitting down on the table, where Gavin was studying a large map of the country spread out before him. " We move to-morrow. A wagon train of more than three thousand four-horse wagons, loaded with money, food, clothing, and ammunition—they say our old acquaintance, the King of Prussia, is devilish short of ammunition—has started from Neisse. If it reaches Olmutz, it will prolong the siege certainly—Frederick thinks it will give him the victory. But if we can stop it, we can save Olmutz without a pitched battle, and thereby ruin the Prussian campaign in the beginning. It has an escort of seven thousand men, and four thousand men will be sent to meet it; that means that the Prussians must lose a whole army corps, as well as their three or four thousand wagons and twelve thousand horses."

"And we will stop them here," cried Gavin, excitably, pointing on the map to the pass of Domstadtl. "You know, that pass, hemmed in by mountains, and narrow and devious, a thousand men could stop ten thousand there."

"We will make a feint at Guntersdorf, a few miles before they get to Domstadtl; but you are right; the Prussians must open that gate and shut it after them if they want to save their convoy; and the opening and shutting will be hard enough, I promise you. We move the day after to-morrow, so go to bed. You will have work to do to-morrow."

Work, indeed, there was to do for every officer and man in Marshal Daun's army; and the morning after they were on the march. It was a bright and beautiful June morning, and it seemed a holiday march to the fifty thousand Austrians. Marshal Daun was noted for keeping his men well fed, and the friendly disposition of the people in the province made this an easy thing to do. The Austrian armies were ever the most picturesque in Europe, owing to the splendour and variety of their uniforms and the different races represented. Rested and refreshed after the disastrous campaign of the autumn, on this day they hailed with joy the prospect of meeting their ancient enemy. With fresh twigs in their helmets, with their knapsacks well filled, the great masses of cavalry, infantry, and artillery stepped out in beautiful order, threading their way along the breezy uplands and through the green heart of the wooded hills down to the charming valleys below.

St. Arnaud and Gavin were with the vanguard. A part of their duty was to throw a reinforcement of eleven hundred men into Olmutz, and it was Marshal Daun's design to make Frederick think that a pitched battle in front of Olmutz was designed.

All through the dewy morning they travelled briskly, and after a short rest at noon they again took up the line of march in the golden afternoon. About six o'clock they reached a little white village in the plain, which was to be the halting place for the night of Loudon's corps.

It was an exquisite June evening, cool for the season, with a young moon trembling in the east, and a sky all green and rose and opal in the west. Myriads of flashing stars glittered in the deep blue heavens, and the passing from the golden light of day to the silver radiance of the night was ineffably lovely.

From the vast green plain and the dusky hills and valleys rose the camp-fires of fifty thousand men. Just at sunset the band of St. Arnaud's regiment, marching out to a green field beyond the village, began to play the national hymn. Other bands, from the near-by plain and the far-away recesses of the hills and valleys, joined in, and the music, deliciously softened by the distances, floated upward, till it was lost in the evening sky.

Gavin and St. Arnaud, walking together along a little hawthorn-bordered lane, listened with a feeling of delight so sharp as to be almost pain. The magic beauty of the scene, the hour, and the sweet music were overpowering. St. Arnaud's words, after a long silence, when the last echo of the music had died among the hills, were:

" And this delicious prelude is the beginning of the great concert of war, cannon, and musketry, the groans and cries of the wounded, the wild weeping of widows and orphans, the tap of the drum in the funeral march."

" And shouts of victory, and the knowledge of having done one's duty, and the sweet acclaims of all we love when we return," answered Gavin.

" I am older than you, and have seen more of war," was St. Arnaud's reply.

Day broke next morning upon a fair and cloudless world. It continued cool for the season, and the sun was not too warm to drive away the freshness of the air. By sunrise they were on the march again, and by noon Frederick, at his great camp of Prossnitz, saw through his glass masses of Austrians appearing through the trees and taking post on the opposite heights, and turning to his aide, said:

" Those Austrians are learning to march, though!"

In the Prussian army it was thought that battle was meant, and troops were hurried forward
to that side of the fortress. But Loudon, stealthily
creeping up on the other side, engaging such force
as was left—eleven hundred grenadiers—without
firing a shot or losing a man double-quicked it
into the fortress. By the afternoon the Austrians
had melted out of sight, and the garrison was
stronger by eleven hundred men.

In this demonstration on the other side of the
fortress St. Arnaud's command had taken part.
It was well understood that the action was a mere
feint to cover the grenadiers who were running
into the fortress, and St. Arnaud had privately
warned Gavin against leading his troop too far,
knowing that a single troop may bring on a general engagement. Gavin promised faithfully to
remember this, and did, until finding himself, for
the first time, close to a small body of Prussian
infantry, in an old apple orchard, he suddenly
dashed forward, waving his sword frantically, and
yelling for his men to come on. The Prussians were
not to be frightened by that sort of thing, and
coolly waiting, partly protected by the trees and
undergrowth, received the Austrians with a vol-
ley. One trooper rolled out of his saddle; the

sight maddened the rest, and the first thing St.
Arnaud knew he was in the midst of a sharp
skirmish. The Prussians stood their ground, and
as the Austrians had no infantry at hand, it took
some time to dislodge them. Nor was it done
without loss on the Austrian side. At last, however, the Prussians began a backward movement,
in perfect order, and without losing a man. St.
Arnaud, glad to have them go on almost any terms,
was amazed and infuriated to hear Gavin shouting
to his men, and to see them following him at a
gallop, under the trees, toward the wall at the
farther end of the orchard, where the Prussians
could ask no better place to make a stand. In
vain the bugler rent the air with the piercing notes
of the recall. Gavin only turned, and waving his
sword at St. Arnaud plunged ahead. St. Arnaud,
wild with anxiety, sent an orderly after him with
peremptory orders to return; but Gavin kept on.
St. Arnaud, sending a number of his men around
in an effort to flank the Prussians, was presently
relieved to see some of Gavin's troopers straggling
back. And last of all he saw Gavin, with a man
lying across the rump of his horse, making his way
out of the orchard. At that moment General Loudon, with a single staff-officer, rode up.

"Captain St. Arnaud," said he in a voice of suppressed anger, "I am amazed at what I see. If this firing is heard, it may bring the Prussians on our backs in such force that not only our grenadiers will not get into the fortress, but they may be captured. My orders were, distinctly, there should be no fighting, if possible. Here I see a part of your command following the enemy into a position where a hundred of them could hold their own against a thousand cavalry."

St. Arnaud was in a rage with Gavin, and thinking it would be the best thing in the world for Gavin to get then and there the rebuke he deserved, replied firmly:

"It is not I, sir, who has disobeyed your orders. Lieutenant Hamilton's impetuosity led him into this, and I have been trying to recall him for the last half hour. Here is Lieutenant Hamilton now."

Gavin rode up. An overhanging bough had grazed his nose and made it bleed, and at the same time had given him a black and swollen eye. And another bough had caught in his coat and torn it nearly off his body. But these minor particulars were lost in the vast and expansive grin which wreathed his face. The thought that illumined

254

his mind and emblazoned his countenance was this:

" The general is here. He must have seen what I did. What good fortune! My promotion is sure."

But what General Loudon said was this:

" Lieutenant Hamilton, your conduct to-day is as much deserving of a court martial as any I ever saw on the field. You have not only unnecessarily endangered the lives of your men—a crime on the part of an officer—but you have come near endangering the whole success of our movement. Your place after this will be with neither the vanguard nor the rear-guard, but with the main body, where you can do as little harm by your rashness as possible."

Gavin's look of triumph changed to one of utter bewilderment, and then to one of mingled rage and horror. General Loudon, without another word, rode off. Gavin, half choking, cried to St. Arnaud:

" But you know what I went after? My first sergeant was shot through both legs—the fellow was in the lead—and he cried out to me to come and save him. Just then I heard the bugle, but could I leave that poor fellow there to die?"

"Certainly not; and this shall be known; but you were very rash in the beginning; so come on, and wash your face the first time you come to water."

The rest of that day was like an unhappy dream to Gavin. They were again on the march by three o'clock, and at bivouac they had rejoined the main body.

Their camp that night was well beyond Olmutz, and led them again toward the mountains. When all the arrangements for the night were made, and their tent was pitched, St. Arnaud, who had been absent for half an hour, returned and looked in. He saw Gavin sitting on the ground in an attitude of utter dejection.

"Come," cried St. Arnaud gayly; "you take the general too seriously; he was angry with you, and so was I, for that matter; but he knows all the facts now."

"It is of no consequence," replied Gavin sullenly. But when St. Arnaud urged him, he rose and joined him for a stroll about the camp. As they were walking along a little path that led along the face of a ravine, they saw, in the clear twilight of the June evening, General Loudon, quite unattended, approaching them. Gavin would have

turned off, but St. Arnaud would not let him. As
they stood on the side of the path, respectfully
to let the general pass, he stopped and said in the
rather awkward way which was usual with him:

" I make no apology for my words to you to-day,
Lieutenant Hamilton, because, on cool reflection,
I still think that you deserve them. I found out,
however, later, that you performed an act of great
gallantry in rescuing your wounded sergeant, and
I have already recommended you for promotion
to Marshal Daun."

General Loudon extended his hand. Gavin,
quite overcome, took it silently, and after a cordial
grasp and a word or two between St. Arnaud and
General Loudon he passed on.

" *You* told him," was all Gavin could say to
St. Arnaud.

" What if I did? I was bound to tell him all
that happened before his report was sent to Marshal Daun."

The day had been a nightmare, but the night
was so happy that Gavin could not sleep.

From the 22d until the 28th Loudon's corps was
travelling toward the convoy by a long and cir-
cuitous hill route, quite out of sight and knowledge
of the Prussians. Marshal Daun had remained

257

17

behind with the main body, having crossed the Moldawa River, while General Ziskowitz, with several thousand men, remained on the other side, ready to reinforce General Loudon, should he be needed.

Those six June days were cloudless, and what with easy marching and mild nights and good fare, never was campaigning pleasanter. Their march lay among the hills and mountains, clothed in their freshest green. Pure and sparkling streams abounded in the wooded heights and cool, green solitudes. The oldest soldiers declared it to be the pleasantest march they had ever made.

On the sixth day they began to listen attentively for the noise of the approaching convoy, which, with its escort, was stretched out full twenty miles. Soon after daybreak, as the Austrians were pushing toward the woody defiles near Guntersdorf, a low reverberation was heard, like the far-distant echo of breakers on the shore. It was the rolling of twelve thousand iron-bound wheels, while the iron-shod hoofs of twelve thousand horses smote the earth. General Loudon immediately made his preparations to attack at Guntersdorf, but it was understood that if a determined resistance was made the Austrians should fall back to Domstadtl, through whose dark defiles and gloomy passes it would be impossible for the Prussians to fight their way.

St. Arnaud's regiment led the van, and he and Gavin rode side by side through the dewy freshness of the morning. The road was steep and winding, but always picturesque, and the trees were in their first fresh livery of green. They rode briskly, men and horses inspired by the freshness and vitality of the delicious mountain air. Ever as they drew nearer the road by which the convoy was making its creaking, rolling, thundering way, the sullen roar grew nearer and louder. On reaching Guntersdorf, General Loudon quickly posted a part of his force in the defiles, with several pieces of artillery concealed among the wooded heights. The general rode hither and thither, and presently came up to where St. Arnaud's and Gavin's regiment was posted, on the brow of a spur of the mountains, thick with trees and rocks.

" We shall meet the advance guard and escort here; it is probably three thousand men, with seven or eight thousand to follow; but if we throw them into confusion and overwhelm them, it will be enough. It is impossible to stop at once a wagon train twenty miles long, and the wagons will help us to win the battle, by those behind pressing those in front upon our guns. Then we shall fall back to Domstadtl, where we can destroy the convoy at our leisure."

At that moment, from their commanding position, St. Arnaud and Gavin looked across a low-lying flank of the mountains, and winding across a valley, four miles away, were a thousand Prussian dragoons, while behind them came a long line of infantry, and then the great wagon train, four abreast.

Never had either Gavin or St. Arnaud seen such a sight as this vast mass of men, horses, and wagons that poured in a steady stream into the valley. The earth shook with the mighty tramp, and great clouds of dust enveloped them like a fog.

The stillness of the early June morning remained unbroken for an hour; yet while this strange procession unwound itself and approached nearer and nearer the defiles of Guntersdorf the noise became deafening, and the horses of the Austrian cavalry trembled with fear as the earth shook under their feet. Presently, the first platoon of Prussian cavalry debouched before an Austrian field battery, concealed in the heights above them.

Suddenly the thunderous roar of wheels and hoofs ` was cut into by the booming of guns, and cannon-balls dropped among the troopers. Instantly there was a halt, the infantry closed up, and under a heavy fire the Prussians formed and rushed up the heights to silence the guns. The Austrians stood their ground, supported by both cavalry and infantry; but meanwhile the wagons were fighting the battle for them. In vain had orders been sent back to halt the train. It came pressing on with an irresistible force, like the force of gravity. The Austrians, seeing the beginning of hopeless confusion and panic in the wagon train, which could only increase, drew off, inducing the Prussians to follow them. There was some sharp fighting among the passes, but, as Gavin said, just as he was beginning to enjoy himself the order came to fall back to Domstadtl.

It was about eight o'clock in the morning when the Austrians began to retrace the road they had travelled soon after daybreak. St. Arnaud's and Gavin's regiment, having had the van in the advance, were the rear-guard of the retrograde movement. As they trotted along behind the last rank of troopers, they both cast many backward looks at the rude mountain roads through which the

Prussians were toiling to their destruction in the impenetrable ravines of Domstadtl. The troops had reformed as well as they could, but the wagons were in a terrible state of disorder. Some hun- dreds of them had stopped at Guntersdorf, but these had been swept away and trampled under foot by the advancing legions. Some of the wagon- ers had turned their vehicles around and were making for the rear, knowing fighting to be ahead of them; others, cutting the traces, mounted the horses and galloped no one knew whither, leaving a solid barricade of wagons in the road to be dis- persed. And ever from behind came this ava- lanche of horses and wagons, pressing on, halting at obstacles, scattered in dire confusion, but always, always, a stream pouring on.

The Austrians reached the gloomy pass of Dom- stadtl only a little in advance of the Prussians, and before they had well taken their positions and unlimbered their artillery the Prussian vanguard, very gallantly led, had forced its way through the pass, with two hundred and fifty wagons on the gallop. But then came the howling of the Aus- trian artillery, and the advance was checked. Col- onel Mosel, the Prussian commander, seeing there was no forcing the pass, formed all his wagons

as fast as they arrived in a great square—a wagon
fortress, as it was called—and prepared to defend
it. General Zeithen, with the guard for the second section, moved rapidly backward to turn the
great stream of men and horses and wheels back
on Troppau. But still they came surging on, men
losing their heads, and driving forward when they
were ordered to turn backward. And on the wagon
fortress played the Austrian artillery, while the
cavalry, dashing up to the remnants of the Prussian guard, sabred them at the wagons. The
wagon horses grew wild with fright, and their
plunging, rearing, and frantic whinnying added
to the maelstrom of disorder. The powder wagons
were in this division, and when an Austrian can-
non-ball fell into one of these, the explosion seemed
as if it would rend the solid mountains. Others
caught from the sparks of this one, and the scene
and sound, as deafening crashes resounded, and
masses of flame and smoke ascended, were like the
infernal regions. Huge rocks, split by the concus-
sion of thousands of pounds of gunpowder, rolled
down the sides of the mountain, sweeping away
men and horses in their resistless course. Up-
rooted trees and a vast mass of débris followed
these awful reverberations. Horses dropped dead

in their tracks, men fell to the ground, stunned by the roar, and were unable to rise; others bled at the nose; some became totally deaf. The sky was obscured with smoke, and in the semi-darkness at midday men's faces, blackened with powder, had a frightful appearance. Fighting continued at all points along the line, where the eleven thousand Prussians endeavoured to make a stand at many places, but were completely overborne. Cannon and musketry added their horrors to the scene, and when men fought at all they fought like demons. All through the June day this fearful combat raged through the mountain passes; and when the sun, obscured in dim clouds, set, the great wagon train was utterly destroyed, with thousands of its escort, wagoners, and horses dead.

Neither St. Arnaud nor Gavin slept in a tent that night, but throwing themselves on the ground, wrapped in their cloaks, slept the sleep of exhaustion and collapse.

By sunset Frederick of Prussia knew that his convoy was destroyed, and with it some of his best troops. That night the bombardment of Olmutz was terrific; the Prussians were firing off the ammunition they could not take away with them. No one slept in the town or the fortress that night for the hurricane of fire and flame that blazed from the Prussian lines. It slackened toward daylight, and when the sun rose there was not a Prussian regiment in sight. The whole army was on the march for the other side of the mountains.

CHAPTER XII

THE abandonment of the siege of Olmutz and the success of the Battle of the Wagons raised to a high pitch the spirits of the Austrian army. Marshal Daun even departed so far from his usual extreme caution as to follow Frederick, who retreated through the mountains, and took up his post upon his own side of them. But he was not suffered to remain in peace, and was continually harassed by the Austrian cavalry and the clouds of Pandours, who followed and hung upon him.

To be of Loudon's corps was enough to say that the summer was one of incessant movement to Gavin Hamilton and St. Arnaud. Both of them were, however, of so much natural activity, that nothing could have suited them better than the constant marching, manœuvring, and fighting of the summer of 1758. It was a particularly cool and healthful summer, and in spite of hard work and soldier's fare, both of them grew more robust than ever.

For Gavin, it was a time as nearly free. from
care and sorrow as often comes on this planet. He
had got his promotion, and blossomed forth as a
full lieutenant. He ardently loved the soldier's
life; he appreciated greatly his extreme good fortune, and although he had but little money, he
required but little while the campaign lasted. It
is true he was beginning to acquire tastes very
much above the rigid poverty in which he had been
reared, and sometimes thought rather ruefully of
the slenderness of his pay if he should be in Vienna the next winter, which he ardently hoped he
would. But with the joyous carelessness of youth,
he considered it settled that as soon as he was
twenty-one, which would be in December, he would
demand his mother's recognition by his father, and
force Sir Gavin to make Lady Hamilton a handsome allowance. Gavin did not trouble himself
very much with the details and difficulties of this·
brilliant scheme, but only figured out how he would
manage to live when it would be no longer necessary for him to divide his scanty pay with his
mother. He sometimes talked about it to St. Arnaud, but St. Arnaud could enlighten him very
little as to his rights under the English laws.
However, it is very easy at twenty, with health and

strength and an officer's commission and a good horse, to throw future perplexities to the winds. This was what Gavin Hamilton did. He was made happy by frequent letters from his mother, who always wrote cheerfully, and to whom, Gavin knew, her present time of rest and peace and hope was blessed. To live upon a little money, and to spend a part of every day in teaching Freda and Gretchen, was no hardship to one who had known Lady Hamilton's sad vicissitudes. Unlike Gavin, she did not look for any redress from Sir Gavin Hamilton for a long time to come. Not until Gavin himself had reached maturity and considerable rank did she think he would be able to enter into a contest for his rights; but it was enough for her to know that she was at last recognized as Sir Gavin Hamilton's lawful wife, and that Gavin was tacitly allowed the position that was his by every right.

In August the battle of Zorndorf had been fought, in which Frederick had very handsomely beaten the Russians under General Fermor, and Marshal Daun, with his usual caution, had fallen back behind Dresden to Stolpen, where he took up, as always, a strong position. There, for four weeks, he faced Frederick, and withstood much provocation to do battle, knowing that every day Frederick's supplies were getting shorter, and the longer the battle was delayed the worse the case of the King of Prussia.

Loudon's corps had the extreme outpost, and barred the road to Bautzen, where the Prussians had their magazines of food and ammunition. During all the month of September there was continual manœuvring and fighting for this road to Bautzen. But General Loudon managed to dispose of all whom Frederick sent against him, until one October day, Frederick himself, with his whole force, took up his march for Bautzen. Then there was great commotion in the whole Austrian army, and in Loudon's corps especially. There was much riding to and fro in the mountain roads and passes, quick mustering of the grenadiers, but it was known tolerably early that the movement was one in force, and that General Loudon could by no means stop it, and could only harass and delay it, which was done with a will. But by sunset the attempt was given over, and it was seen that the next move in the game must be by Marshal Daun with his whole army.

Toward night, as Gavin and St. Arnaud were making ready to bivouac with their men, General

Loudon and his staff rode by. The general stopped and beckoned to Gavin.

"Your horse appears to be fresh," said he, "and I wish to send a last dispatch to Marshal Daun to-night. Take a small escort, and carry this to Stolpen as quickly as possible. You should be able to bring me a reply before daylight to-morrow morning. Marshal Daun will provide you with fresh horses;" and tearing a leaf out of his pocket-book, and using his hat for a writing-desk, he scribbled a few lines in pencil, addressed them to Marshal Daun, and rode on.

It did not take Gavin five minutes to mount and be off, with a couple of troopers trotting behind him. The night was falling, and it grew dark in the mountain fastnesses; but so much had Gavin and his men ridden over those tortuous and rocky roads in the last few weeks, that not only they, but their horses, knew the way perfectly. They rode on steadily, occasionally meeting with returning couriers; but by nine o'clock they seemed to be the only travellers on the road. They were passing through a dense woodland, hemmed in on each side of the road by rocky walls, when suddenly a small party of men appeared in their path, swiftly and silently, as shadows rising from the earth.

Gavin had no apprehension of an enemy, and supposed he was meeting a belated party of Austrians.
This was confirmed when the person, apparently
an officer, at the head of the number, rode up to
Gavin, and said:

" I presume that you are an officer, and going
toward Stolpen."

" You are right," answered Gavin, trying to
make out in the half darkness the uniform of the
person addressing him.

" Then, may I ask you to deliver a letter to
Marshal Daun? I am not at liberty to say from
whom it is, but it will be a favour to Marshal Daun
if you can contrive it into his hands."

Gavin hesitated for a moment as the stranger
drew a letter from his breast; and then, to
Gavin's infinite surprise, threw the letter on the
ground, and the whole party galloped off. One
of Gavin's troopers, dismounting, picked the letter
up, and striking his flint, the address was easily
read. It was to his Excellency, Field-Marshal
Daun.

Then followed a correct enumeration of Marshal
Daun's titles and honours. And at the very first
glance Gavin recognized the handwriting of Frederick of Prussia. To make sure, he took from his

breast pocket the treasured memorandum, which he always carried, that Frederick had given him the night of their adventure at Breslau. Yes, it was impossible to mistake that handwriting, and there was not the smallest attempt to disguise it on the mysterious letter. Gavin returned both to his safest pocket, and rode on steadily.

At one o'clock in the morning he and his two troopers clattered into the camp at Stolpen. He was at once shown to Marshal Daun's headquarters, a peasant's hut, in which a light was burning and a couple of hard-worked aides-de-camp were busy at a writing-table.

" The marshal has just gone into the inner room, but left orders that he should be aroused at once, should any dispatches come from General Loudon," said one of them.

The marshal, however, saved them the trouble, for, hearing voices in the outer room, he appeared at the rude door that separated the rooms. He had lain down wrapped in his cloak, and it still hung about him.

Politely motioning Gavin to sit, he opened and read General Loudon's dispatch, and promptly dictated a reply to his aide. When that was done, Gavin handed him the mysterious letter he had received, briefly recounting the circumstances under which he received it.

Marshal Daun read it attentively, and then, laying it down on the table, said with a puzzled air:

" This is very strange. This letter appears to be a reply to a letter I wrote General Fermor before the battle of Zorndorf, warning him against rashly engaging the King of Prussia, and expressing my high opinion of the King as a military man. I have had no word of reply to it until now, and this letter is not in General Fermor's handwriting. I will read it to you.

" ' Your Excellency was in the right to warn me against a cunning enemy whom you knew better than I. Here have I tried fighting him and got beaten. Your unfortunate   FERMOR.' "

Gavin, taking Frederick's letter from his pocket, silently laid it before the marshal, and Marshal Daun, after reading it, passed it over to his aides. A universal grin went around, not even excepting the grave and ceremonious field-marshal, at poor General Fermor's expense.

" Well," said Marshal Daun, after a moment, " the King of Prussia is entitled to his pleasantry. And I am sincerely glad he knows that I am incapable of one of the greatest faults of a soldier—

underrating the enemy. I ever considered that king, since first I had the honour of fighting him, as one of the great masters of the art of war, and I have no objection to his knowing it. General Fermor did not know it, and behold, he was beaten at Zorndorf."

There was no time to be lost in returning, and fresh horses being already provided, within half an hour Gavin was on his way back to General Loudon. As he rode along in the darkness, and then in the gray dawn, he could not help laughing at Frederick's grim humour. Clearly, he had taken some trouble to get his reply conveyed to Marshal Daun, and Gavin had no doubt that the troopers who had delivered it to him were really Prussians, disguised. By daylight he had got to General Loudon's headquarters, and after delivering his dispatches went to the hut of boughs in which St. Arnaud and himself spread their blankets. He was very tired, but before lying down to sleep he told St. Arnaud about the King of Prussia's letter.

"How like the elfish nature of the man!" was St. Arnaud's comment.

The utmost activity prevailed in the Austrian ranks after Frederick's escape, and it became known through that telepathy which anticipates great events that a general engagement was impending; and when on the night of the 5th of October, in the midst of a drenching rain, wild wind, and pitch darkness, the whole Austrian army abandoned Stolpen, and took up its march for Kittlitz, a strong position east of Bautzen and of Hochkirch, around which was collected the whole of the King of Prussia's army, all knew that the hour was at hand.

So secretly was this done, that, although it was known that the Austrian army was on the move, it was with the greatest surprise that, on the evening of the 10th of October, Frederick, reaching Hochkirch, found Marshal Daun securely established with ninety thousand men in lines many miles long on the woody heights that surround the hill upon which the village of Hochkirch—of immortal memory—stands. Frederick had but his forty thousand, and the amazement of the Austrians was as great as their delight when they saw this mighty captain, usually so wise in the disposition of his armies, walk into a ring encircled by his enemies, and then quietly sit down before them.

A part of Loudon's corps was encamped on a wooded crest, the Czarnabog, or Devil's Mountain, as the village people called it, and among them was the regiment of St. Arnaud and Gavin. It was a lovely, still, autumn afternoon when the two, standing together at the highest point of the mountain, saw the mass of Prussians coming into sight . on the opposing heights, divided only by the Lobau water, and the many streams and brooks that go to make up the Spree. As it became plain that the dark masses of approaching men were Prussians, St. Arnaud and Gavin, standing in a group of other officers, could not conceal their surprise.

"This king must be mad," said St. Arnaud. Gavin nodded, and continued to watch the Prussians, as a post for several thousand of them was being marked out not half a mile distant from the heights, dense with trees, where thousands of Austrians, with several batteries of heavy guns, were placed.

Numbers of Prussian officers were seen moving about as the various regiments marched in, and at last a group on horseback appeared, in which was a figure that St. Arnaud and Gavin instantly recognized without glasses. Worn, thin, and wizened as he was, Frederick of Prussia was ever an imposing figure. All who saw that slight, pale man, shabbily dressed, but splendidly mounted, riding nonchalantly into the view of tens of thousands of men, were thrilled at the sight of him. Here was one of the world's masters and dictators. Beaten he might be, he was never conquered; less in force than his enemy, he was always dangerous; with but a thousand men behind him, he could yet keep his enemies awake at night. He rode to the edge of the plateau on which the village is built, and surveyed the long lines of his enemies drawn up for many miles in the woods, and hills, and hollows close by. The sun was sinking in a blaze of glory, and its mellow light fell upon a landscape singularly beautiful. In a long, deep valley ran a rapid and musical stream, with many branches. White villages nestled among the hills, and the blue air was pierced by slender church steeples. A thin haze, from many thousands of camp-fires, enveloped the valleys in mysterious beauty, and the white tents, in tens of thousands, lay like snow-flakes on the still green earth. No eye noted this, though, as long as Frederick of Prussia remained in sight, his slight, compact figure on his horse silhouetted against the evening sky. Suddenly from the wooded heights, directly in front of him, a flash and a roar burst forth, and twenty Austrian cannon-balls ploughed up the ground. The King's horse stood motionless—the charger that

carried Frederick the Great must needs be used
to cannon and musketry fire—and Frederick himself, without changing his position, put his field-
glass to his eyes, and coolly surveyed the scene.
A dozen officers galloped toward him, but Frederick with a gesture motioned them away. Five minutes of perfect silence followed. Of the thousands
who beheld him, every man held his breath; and
when a second round roared out, a kind of universal groan and shudder ran like electricity through
the watching multitudes. This time it threw some
earth upon the King, and then, calmly dusting it
off, he turned and rode toward the village church.
Ten minutes after, Gavin and St. Arnaud eagerly
watching, he appeared upon the little belfry. Twilight was falling, though, and it was no longer possible to see clearly. Lights were twinkling, and
the blaze of the camp-fires became lurid in the falling darkness. In a little while silence but for the
sentry's tread, and darkness but for the camp-fires
burning through the chill autumn night, had settled down upon the scene.

The next morning rose clear and beautiful, and
daylight only showed more plainly the extreme
danger of Frederick's position. It was known,
however, through spies, that it would be impossi-

ble for him to leave for several days, owing to a
lack of provisions and ammunition upon any road
that he might take. The Austrians wished to lull
him into security, and three days were spent in
what seemed to the Prussians preparations to defend themselves on the part of the Austrians. The
air resounded with thousands of axes hewing trees,
to form abatis; slight earthworks were thrown up,
and Marshal Daun gave every sign of preparing to
defend himself rather than to attack. He even
continued to have false information sent Frederick,
that the Austrians were preparing to fall back on
Zittau. But at nightfall, on Friday, the 13th of
October, thirty thousand Austrians stole away,
leaving their camp-fires brightly burning, and en-
closing Frederick on the only side he had been
free, rendered his escape impossible, except by
cutting his way through.

St. Arnaud's and Gavin's regiment were kept
concealed in the Devil's Mountains. Wild beyond
expression were these hills, with vast boulders,
black hollows, trees standing so close that daylight
scarcely penetrated, and tangled thickets. In these
dark hills three thousand men were easily hidden.
Through these thick wildernesses were cut roads
for the ammunition wagons.

The night of the 13th of October was moonless and starless. The fair days preceding had been followed by a day of dun clouds and brown fog. During the dark and rainy night, when the silent movement of thirty thousand Austrians, under Marshal Daun himself, had taken place, the three thousand grenadiers and light troops of Loudon's corps, encamped in the Devil's Mountains, had peacefully spent the night. At four o'clock they were to be called by their officers, without blare of the trumpet; and when the clock in the belfry of the village church of Hochkirch struck five they were to fall upon the Prussians. Gavin and St. Arnaud, having to be awake early, did not sit up late, but wrapped in their cloaks, with their saddles for pillows, lay down before a roaring fire, which was to be kept up all night, and were soon asleep.

At three o'clock St. Arnaud rose. It was pitch dark but for the ruddy blaze of the fire still burning, and a cold, brown mist hid everything from sight except the ring of light from the fire. Gavin was still sleeping—he always slept until he was roused.

The orderly was already preparing something savoury in an iron pan, and when it was ready St.

Arnaud gave Gavin a vigorous shake, which brought him to his feet at once. Without losing a moment he fell to upon the contents of the pan; for there was no hour of the day or night that Gavin Hamilton was not ready to eat and to fight.

"Bad for the Prussians, this fog," he said between mouthfuls of bacon and cheese.

"Very," laconically replied St. Arnaud, who was not half the trencher-man that Gavin was.

Their horses were already fed and saddled, and in a few minutes they were on horseback, going through the ranks of soldiers, who were munching their breakfasts while the horses munched their hay.

At half-past four o'clock, when it was still perfectly dark, the Austrians were ready and ranked and waiting for the church clock to toll five. It seemed a long wait, and St. Arnaud noticed Gavin blinking his eyes with sleep as he sat on his horse. Presently, through the white mist which wrapped the world for them, echoed five delicate, light strokes of the clock on the village hill, and immediately after the silvery sound of the Prussian bugles sounded faintly through the fog.

And then came a sudden deafening roar of artillery, a crashing of musketry from many thousand muskets, and in an instant of time the Prussians were surrounded by a ring of fire five miles in circumference.

By that time St. Arnaud's and Gavin's regiment was picking its way out of the woods, toward the village of Winschke, where it was to support the grenadiers. As they came into the open country the impenetrable mist lay over the whole earth; but it was lighted up at every moment, and in a vast circle, by the blaze of gunpowder. Across the valley, by the constant flashes they could see great masses of Austrian cavalry dashing themselves upon the Prussian infantry, which was completely surprised. The Prussians in the village were awake, too, and the Austrians were pouring in upon them. The thunder of the artillery, the sharp crash of musketry, the shouts and cries, rang through the hills and valleys, where a hundred and thirty thousand men were fighting.

It was trying work, standing still at the brow of the hill, waiting for the word to charge down the hill, ford the little river, and up the steep incline to the village. All around them was fighting— masses of Austrians, horse and foot, throwing themselves upon the Prussians, who were outnumbered two to one, but making a stiff defence and commanded by the greatest captain of the age.

" I wonder what kind of a humour the King was in this morning when he was waked by our pounding him ? " asked Gavin of St. Arnaud.

" He was not waked, that you may depend upon. He was no doubt up and on horseback by five o'clock. But his headquarters are two miles away, and it must have taken him some little time to form a plan of defence, for he could not tell at first that he was being attacked on all sides at once."

" It is said that when Marwitz, his adjutant, was called upon to mark off the post Tuesday evening, he flatly refused to do it, saying he would have no part in marking off a post so dangerous, and the King promptly ordered him under arrest."

" He was to get away from here this afternoon, only Marshal Daun was, for once, beforehand with him—a—a—ah ! " for at this a Prussian battery wheeled in front of them and opened up with vigour.

" Forward ! " rang out, and the regiment moved as if on parade, the trot down hill increasing to a gallop up the hill, after they had crossed the stream.

From that on Gavin saw nothing of the battle except the furious mêlée just around him. The Prussians held the village stubbornly, and with a battery of artillery and a few regiments of infantry stood like rocks, while the Austrians poured infantry and cavalry upon them. Gavin, at the head of his troop, dashed again and again at the Prussian lines, only to be repulsed. He heard himself as in a dream shouting:

" Come on! Their ammunition can't last forever! "

And as the Austrians came on, an endless, steady stream, never ceasing, he saw riding out of the mist, which was slowly melting before the rising sun, the figure of the King of Prussia. He dashed among the struggling Prussian infantry, and as if by magic a line of bayonets was formed around him, against which the Austrians threw themselves like an avalanche of fire and steel. Then came a Titanic struggle, men, guns, and horses inextricably mixed, no man having time to load and fire, but steel to steel, sabres and bayonets, and a fearful and hideous din drowning the roar of cannon and shriek of musketry. No man asked or gave quarter, but with powder-blackened faces and grim eyes and distorted features sought death or gave it.

It lasted a short ten minutes, but it seemed hours. Gavin Hamilton, in the midst of it, whirling his sabre like a flail, found himself, he knew not how, on the ground, with his riderless horse plunging wildly near him, a forest of Austrian bayonets behind him, and a steady line of Prussian steel in front of him. Sometimes that line wavered, sometimes it broke, but it always formed again. And suddenly the line of glittering steel parted for a moment, and he saw the King of Prussia for one moment erect on his horse, and the next the horse staggered and fell, and Gavin, running forward, with his strong left arm seized Frederick by the arm, shrieking:

"You took me prisoner once; now it is my turn!"

Their eyes met for one brief instant, and the glance that Frederick gave him made Gavin forget the battle, the uproar, the danger—all, except those steel-blue eyes, sparkling with the light of battle; that slight, wiry figure, with one uplifted arm, and the singular music of that voice, ringing out above the shouting and the clash of arms:

"Not yet! Not yet!"

The ancient Germans represented their god of war as huge, blonde, and bearded; Gavin Hamilton would have said that Frederick of Prussia, unhorsed, defeated, and almost captured, was the ideal of the lord of battles.

In another moment a regiment of Prussian hussars appeared as if they had sprung out of the ground, their horses plunging over every obstacle, their sabres flashing right and left; and encircling the King, he was swept out of sight like magic. It was over in the twinkling of an eye—one instant Gavin had Frederick by the arm, looking into his blue and blazing eyes; the next instant there was a trampling of iron hoofs, a flashing of steel, a torrent of men, and Gavin had dropped to his knees without so much as feeling a blow. Only everything grew suddenly indistinct and far away, and then he knew no more.

It seemed to him but another instant before he revived, perfectly alive to everything, but it was strangely quiet after the fierce confusion of the last charge. There was still fighting going on, but it was far at the other end of the village, and elsewhere it seemed to be quite over. He opened his eyes, and glanced upward; the mist was rolling off the valleys, and the sun, shining in unclouded splendour, was high in the heavens. It must be at least nine o'clock, thought Gavin, and he knew it was not more than six when the order to charge was given. He concluded that he had been knocked on the head by a Prussian musket or a horse's hoof. Glancing around again, he saw himself in a pool of blood. A dozen men lay in ghastly attitudes near him, and within touch of his hand was a dead horse. Gavin recognized the horse—it was the one ridden by the King of Prussia.

He grew faint presently, and concluded it was the neighbourhood of the horse; he tried to get up and walk away, which he failed to accomplish, and knew no more. When he next came to himself, he was lying in a little cart jolting along the road, and his head was aching miserably. He was in the open country, and the stars were shining overhead. It was very cold, and St. Arnaud was holding his head and trying to wrap him the better in cloaks. Gavin made quite sure before he spoke; then he said:

"St. Arnaud, is the King of Prussia a prisoner?"

"No. As well try to take the devil prisoner as that man."

A pause.

"But for the wound in my head I could have done it. I had my hand on him."

" It would take ten thousand men like you to carry off that Frederick of Prussia. The Prussian hussars did for you and the rest of our poor fellows very handsomely."

" Yes; this wound in my head "—

" You have no wound in your head."

" But I have, I tell you. It makes me suffer terribly."

" The wound is in your leg. It is broken, but the surgeons have set it, and I am taking you to Zittau. There you can be treated, and I shall return to the regiment."

" Yes; it is in my leg; I know it now. Did I lose my sword ? "

" No; you were holding it tightly when I found you."

" So you came to look after me ? "

" Certainly. Everything was over, and what was left of the Prussians in full retreat before ten o'clock."

" Are the Prussians really beaten ? "

" As much as they ever are. Frederick will be up and at us again in a month as if he had never been beaten at all. But he has lost Marshal Keith. The marshal's body was found among a heap of slain, watched by a foot-soldier, an Englishman,

288

who had it carried into the church. And there General Lacy recognized the grand old marshal. General Lacy wept at the sight. The marshal will be buried to-morrow with full military honours, as if he were an Austrian marshal, General Lacy acting as chief mourner. Frederick has no more Keiths among his generals."

Gavin broke out into a cry, so terrible was the jolting of the wagon upon his wounded leg.

Presently, when he became calmer, he asked:

"Will my leg be crooked or disfigured in any way if I get well?"

"Pooh! I don't know. It is no matter, so you get well."

"But my legs are very important to me, at least."

"You are very vain of them. Well, I dare say they will be all right."

Hours of agony followed, and Gavin was not of the sort to endure pain silently. He moaned and cried incessantly, and St. Arnaud comforted him as a mother comforts a suffering child.

By daylight he was at Zittau, lying in a rude bed in an artisan's house. St. Arnaud stayed with him a few hours, and then was obliged to leave him, but not before sending an express to Vienna to Lady Hamilton, to Gavin's joy and relief. He felt, as he lay in agonizing pain upon his hard bed, that could he but know his mother was near, half his suffering would be over.

Six days of suffering followed, suffering that turned his ruddy cheeks to a deathly pallor, and brought lines never to be effaced in his boyish face. He burned with fever, while racked with anguish, and neither day nor night brought him any relief. The artisan's family were kind to him, and he had the surgical attention necessary, but Zittau was full of wounded Austrians, and all suffered hardships.

On the sixth evening, just as Gavin felt himself sinking into delirium, the door to his little room opened. He thought it was the woman of the house coming to do what little she could for him; but oh, happiness! it was his mother; and behind her was thirteen-year-old Freda, lugging a great soft pillow; and Gavin, throwing his arms around his mother's neck as she clasped him, sobbed and cried with joy and pain as he had not done since he was a little lad.

His mother, to soothe him, told him the circumstances of her coming to him.

" As soon as I had that dear St. Arnaud's letter,

Madame Ziska and Count Kalenga got the money for my journey, and they insisted I should not start alone, and would have me take Freda, who is worth ten grown women for helpfulness. The Empress Queen herself sent me a message, saying you were at Zittau; and Prince Kaunitz gave me a letter enabling me to get post-horses anywhere on the road. So here we are, to stay until you can be moved to Vienna."

The pain was no better for many days, but it was incomparably easier for Gavin to bear, with his mother's tender ministrations and Freda's untiring help, who was ever at hand to do, with the greatest intelligence, whatever was to be done. With all of Gavin's youth and strength, it was yet six weeks before he could be moved to Vienna by easy stages. It was not an unhappy six weeks. The Austrians were in high spirits, and that was of great advantage in the convalescence of all the wounded. Gavin received early assurances of promotion and a good command as soon as the spring campaign opened. He, however, was not a conspicuously good patient, but rather the other way. He not only required to be nursed, but to be entertained, and in this last particular his mother's natural gifts and accomplishments were invaluable.

In return for all that she could do, however, Gavin would occasionally long for St. Arnaud's charming society, and was far from polite in expressing his wishes. When he grew intolerable his mother would quietly withdraw, and let him get over his fit of ill humour as best he could. Little Freda, on the contrary, would be more tender and attentive the less he deserved it, and rewarded, rather than punished, his spells of diabolism.

When Gavin was able to sit up, he found diversion in keeping up the English lessons with Freda that Lady Hamilton had begun. The first sign of his return to his old self was one day when she discovered that he was teaching the innocent Freda the most outlandish pronunciation of English words, and laughing uproariously at her.

" I should think a young gentleman who calls his own name Ameeltone would try to mend his own pronunciation instead of imposing on Freda, who can say Hamilton quite well," was Lady Hamilton's comment.

In December, after a slow journey, Gavin found himself in his old quarters again, to the delight of his mother and his good friends. He was not yet able to attend the Empress Queen's levee, but an aide-de-camp of the Emperor's had come to make formal inquiry concerning him and to bring a kind message from the sovereigns.

In December was Gavin's twenty-first birthday, and to his great delight he found that St. Arnaud, then in winter quarters at Olmutz, would come to Vienna for a short visit about that time. On the winter afternoon that St. Arnaud arrived Gavin threw aside his crutches. It was his twenty-first birthday.

Madame Ziska had arranged a little feast for them, and Lady Hamilton, who had taken the utmost interest in it, had gone out with Freda to attend to some of the preparations. St. Arnaud arrived at five o'clock, and a few minutes after Freda returned alone, with a letter. She ran upstairs, and with a pale, scared face handed it to Gavin. It ran thus:

" I have this moment heard that your father is ill with smallpox and deserted by all his servants. I am going to him. I forbid you to come to the house, from the danger of infection not only to yourself, but to the family of our friends. You may, however, come to-morrow morning and every morning at nine o'clock to the corner of the street, and if all goes well I will be at the middle window in the second story with a white handkerchief in my hand. If I should never see you again, be always a good man, and do not cease to love your devoted mother.   M. HAMILTON."

Gavin, weakened by his illness, fell back in his chair, faint and overcome. St. Arnaud had to do the questioning of little Freda, who, though much frightened, could yet give a very intelligent account of what had happened.

"We were coming out of a shop," she said, "when a man, looking like a servant, came up to us, and catching Lady Hamilton by the sleeve, begged her to go to a house not far off, where he said Sir Gavin Hamilton lay dying of smallpox, and quite alone. Lady Hamilton trembled very much at that, and asked him why he had deserted his master. The man answered that he had a wife and children, and when all the other servants left he was afraid to stay; and then it came out—for the man did not at first tell it—that he had left Sir Gavin the day before, and had gone for a doctor, but did not know whether the doctor went to Sir Gavin or not. But the man felt troubled about his master, and knowing about Lady Hamilton, had followed her up, and watched for her to come out of the shop. Then Lady Hamilton, weeping very much, went back into the shop, and wrote this letter, and brought me to the corner of our street, and kissing me good-by, went off with the man."

Gavin started up, crying out:

" I must go at once to my mother ! " but sank back, exhausted; and St. Arnaud, seeing the necessity for quieting him, said:

" I will go to the house, which I know well, and try to attract Lady Hamilton's attention, and perhaps I can find out something."

He went immediately, and returned in half an hour. He found Gavin much agitated, and Madame Ziska and Freda vainly trying to calm him. The news St. Arnaud brought was not, however, calculated to soothe poor Gavin.

" I went straight to the house—one of the finest in the court quarter," he said. " It was not necessary to know that the house had been hastily abandoned. Doors and even windows were wide open, and Sir Gavin's dog, a huge mastiff, lay moaning with hunger on the stairs of the main entrance, for the servants fled yesterday. There was but a solitary light in the whole vast place—I suppose, in Sir Gavin's room. I stood on the street below, and threw pebbles at a window, until Lady Hamilton appeared at the window of a lower room. 'He is very ill,' she said, 'and I believe would not have lived through another night had I not come. He is now delirious.' I asked her if Sir Gavin's valet had sent her a doctor. She replied the doctor had not yet come. At that moment the doctor arrived, on foot. I noticed that his man, following with his medicine case, was deeply pitted with smallpox, and I asked the doctor if, for a handsome consideration, I could engage this man to assist Lady Hamilton, which he agreed to, after making sure that Sir Gavin was of the rank and position to pay well for all that was done for him. So that she is now provided with help. I remained outside until Lady Hamilton again appeared at the window. She was weeping, and told me the doctor thought Sir Gavin could hardly survive many hours."

"Why should my mother weep for that man, who has made her whole life wretched; and why—ah, why should she risk her life for him?" cried Gavin, throwing himself about in his chair in his agony of grief and alarm.

"Because," quietly replied St. Arnaud, "she loves him still. I have seen it always. Your mother, Gavin, is one of those faithful women, whose love once given cannot be withdrawn; who silently and patiently endure to the end, and whose unshaken constancy makes one admire and despair. In one moment of Sir Gavin's danger she forgot twenty-one years of insults and injuries."

" I cannot understand it," sighed Gavin.

" Nor can I. Only exalted souls like hers can. But I tell you a fact, which I have seen in Lady Hamilton's eyes ever since the first moment I saw her, that Sir Gavin Hamilton has never ceased to be dear to her, although her pride forbade her to acknowledge it. There could be no doubt of it to-night when, sobbing and trembling, she told me that in his delirium he raved of her and his child as they were twenty years ago, and moaned that his wife would not come to him. She sent you her dearest love and prayers, and only begged, if you valued her happiness, to keep away from the infection. She will talk to you from the window, as she did to me; it is some distance from the ground."

The birthnight supper was a very different affair from what had been planned. Although all tried to cheer Gavin, and make him hopeful of the best, all of them were oppressed with fear. Lady

Hamilton's life was in jeopardy every hour. Gavin slept not at all that night, and soon after sunrise was standing with a forlorn face under his mother's window. He looked listlessly at the splendid façade, the marble steps, the tall, bronze lamps, all the evidences of wealth, and wondered stupidly at the good and evil in human nature, which made all desert Sir Gavin in his hour of direst need except the one human being he had most injured.

Not until nine o'clock did Lady Hamilton appear at the window.

" He still lives," she said.

It was in Gavin's heart to say that he cared not whether Sir Gavin lived or died if but she escaped; but he dared not.

" Mother," cried Gavin, " I have not slept since your letter came, and I have been here since sunrise."

", My poor, poor Gavin! Would you break your mother's heart by making yourself ill? Go home now, and do not come back until to-morrow at nine."

" Mother, I shall go mad if I do not see you again this day. Let me come at sunset. I *will* come, and I will stand on this pavement un-

til you speak to me, if it is until to-morrow
morning."

" Well, then, at sunset, dearest."

Days of agonizing suspense followed for Gavin.
He learned in that time to know that, fearful as
bodily pain is, it is a bed of roses to mental anguish. All he had suffered with his wounds was
nothing to what he endured in those December
days when his mother remained in the infected
house. Sir Gavin, after a week of the extremest
danger, began to hold his own, and then to gain
a little and a little. This change was plain in every
tone of Lady Hamilton's voice, and in every linea-
ment of her pale, glorified face. It amazed and
confounded Gavin, but it waked no jealousy in his
heart. His nature was too large, too free, too lib-
eral, to let a shade come between his mother and
himself. He knew that she had once loved his
father well; and when he came to examine his
memory he could not recall a single expression of
resentment she had ever used against Sir Gavin.
True, she had approved Gavin on each of the two
occasions when he had resented his father's treatment of her, but Gavin felt that in strict justice
she must have approved him, and it would have
been a fatal mistake for him to have acted other-

wise. But though convinced of Sir Gavin's wickedness of conduct, she could not wholly withdraw the memory of her love, and at the first need of her it rose again, full of life and vitality.

It was eight weeks before Sir Gavin was entirely well and it was safe to enter the house. But on a bright and spring-like February day Gavin was to be allowed to see his mother. Lady Hamilton had especially asked that St. Arnaud and Madame Ziska come with him. She knew her own power over Gavin, but she was not quite sure of his resistance, and knowing well that both of these noble souls would be on her side, she thought it well to have them at hand.

Arrived at the house, a striking change was visible in its aspect from the day that its master lay ill and deserted to the time when he was again the Sir Gavin Hamilton of old. A splendidly liveried porter opened the great carved door, and within four powdered and silk-stockinged footmen obsequiously showed them into a noble drawing-room. But Gavin saw nothing except his mother, flitting down the grand staircase as the door opened; and bounding up three steps at the time, he caught her in his strong, young arms, and covered her face with kisses. And then, holding her

off at arm's length, he studied her countenance,
thinking to find her thin and pallid. But instead,
he had never seen her face so round, so delicately
rosy, so nearly beautiful. Lady Hamilton's examination of him was not nearly so satisfactory.

"My poor, poor Gavin!" she said, and tears
sprung to her eyes. Gavin had not endured six
weeks of bodily pain and eight weeks of the anguish of fear without showing it.

After a few grateful words to Madame Ziska
and St. Arnaud, Lady Hamilton turned and said
with authority to Gavin:

"You will now go with me to your father's
room."

Gavin, obeying the habit of years, went with his
mother silently. His mind was in a tumult. He
had hated his father very deeply ever since he could
remember, nor was he capable of the sublime self-
forgetfulness of his mother; for he not only bitterly resented his mother's injuries, but his own.
He, the son of a man rich, powerful, and well
born, had spent his youth in poverty, in ignorance
of many things, in the hardship of a private soldier's lot. No; he could never forgive his father.
He was saying this to himself when his mother
stopped before a large door, and spoke.

" Sir Gavin is changed—more changed than I could have believed. And this change was not brought about for any advantage to be gained; it is that, looking death in the face, his better self was heard. He told me almost in the first days that he was conscious he always yearned over you as other fathers yearn over their sons, and at the very time he tried to win you from me he felt ten times the longing for you when you showed a spirit loyal to your mother. Sir Gavin, with all his faults, is not the man to miss the point of honour, and he respects that in you. He says often to me, whenever we speak of you, ' The boy is no poltroon.' "

" But what, mother," asked Gavin, firmly, " of his treatment of you ? "

" That is between us, and with it you have nothing to do," replied Lady Hamilton, with a flush rising to her face. " It is enough to know that Sir Gavin will do all he can to atone "—

" Atone ! " cried Gavin, wheeling around and bringing his fist down on the wainscoting in a burst of rage.

The door opened noiselessly, and Sir Gavin Hamilton, dreadfully changed in appearance, but with the same indomitable coolness, appeared.

"The boy is right," he said, turning to Lady Hamilton. "Men talk of atonement; how imperfect must it ever be! This boy hates me; it may be long before he feels otherwise. But for myself, I do not hate him, and never hated him. I should have despised him, though, had he accepted the conditions I offered him."

"Yet you offered them," replied Gavin; "you offered me anything and everything if I would abandon my mother."

Sir Gavin waved his hand calmly.

"That is past," he said. "She saved my life at the risk of her own. I have offered her the only recompense possible. I will acknowledge her to be my wife. Of course, in doing that, I am condemning my own course for twenty years past. Well, men sometimes do that. It is not in me to fall down on my knees and ask the world to flagellate me. I make neither promises nor professions. I only offer to regard the imperfect marriage ceremony which united us as perfectly valid. We both acted in good faith. The time came when I would have been glad to have been free from the bond. I shall make no further effort. I cannot, in fact, after having received her in my house, and acknowledged her right to be here."

THE LIVELY ADVENTURES

It was not gracious, but, as Sir Gavin truly said, it was not in him to abase himself.

Lady Hamilton's reply was made with the utmost dignity.

" I ask nothing but the recognition of my right and my son's right. I do not desire to remain in this house an hour longer than is necessary to establish the fact in the eyes of the world that I am Lady Hamilton. Then I shall go with my son and depend entirely upon him and upon myself. He has never yet failed me either in respect or affection, and having secured his right, I have nothing more to ask."

Never in all his life had Gavin felt prouder of his mother than at that moment. Even a gleam of admiration came into Sir Gavin Hamilton's cold eyes. His reply was more conciliatory than anything he had yet said.

" I do not feel I have the right to exercise any compulsion over you, madam, but I would suggest that you remain in my house until I am sufficiently recovered to attend you to the royal levee. That will be the simplest as well as the most effective method of undoing the work of many years."

Lady Hamilton bowed silently, and Gavin, with a formal inclination of the head to his father, offered his mother his arm, and they descended the stairs.

Sir Gavin, with a strange expression on his face, watched them as they descended, and when they reached the first landing, supposing themselves unseen, mother and son fell into each other's arms and clung together. But Sir Gavin Hamilton stood watching—watching, while that which did duty for him as a heart was deeply stirred.

Below were Madame Ziska and St. Arnaud. St. Arnaud was just saying:

"I am getting frightened, they are so quiet; Gavin must have thrown his father out of the window," when Lady Hamilton and Gavin appeared.

"What did Gavin do?" anxiously cried Madame Ziska.

"All I could have asked of him," replied his mother. She did not say all she could have wished. She had hoped that he would offer his hand to his father, but he had not done it. However, glad to have gained so much from him, Lady Hamilton would not be too exacting. And Madame Ziska, by way of encouraging Gavin, said what she did not feel:

"What a sweet, forgiving Gavin is it!" and patted his shoulder.

Lady Hamilton then said simply that she would remain until after the next levee, which she would attend with Sir Gavin.

"And then you will come back to us," cried Gavin.

"If you do not come here," said St. Arnaud, out of Gavin's hearing, and exchanging glances with Madame Ziska.

Lady Hamilton led them through the splendid lower floor, the bewigged and bepowdered footmen obsequiously showing the way, and at the same time indicating they knew who was mistress there. On parting, Gavin promised faithfully to return the next day.

Gavin expected to be met with many urgings from St. Arnaud and Madame Ziska and Count Kalenga to be more conciliatory to his father, but they wisely said nothing. Every day Gavin went to see his mother, and every day, when he saw her the acknowledged mistress of his father's house, it seemed as if his hatred to Sir Gavin was abating little by little. On the third day he met Sir Gavin as he was about to go out in his coach, and heard him say:

"Make my compliments to Lady Hamilton, and ask for the honour of her company to drive."

The footman disappeared and returned.

"Lady Hamilton sends her compliments, and regrets she cannot accept Sir Gavin's invitation. She is expecting Lieutenant Hamilton."

Sir Gavin looked so cross and surprised that Gavin could not restrain a grin—he had never been able to smile at anything his father did before.

All this had not been unknown in Vienna society, and curiosity was at the highest pitch the night of the royal levee, when the strangely reconciled couple were to appear for the first time in public. Gavin and St. Arnaud were to be present—their first appearance after the campaign in which both had distinguished themselves. On the next day both were to return to their command at Olmutz. As they rolled along in a hired coach toward the royal palace St. Arnaud said:

"How happy you should be! How I envy you!"

Gavin was surprised at this. St. Arnaud was always cheerful, even gay, self-contained, and Gavin had thought a very happy man.

"Why should I not envy you? Compare your youth with mine."

"True. But I have no one in the world to love or to love me. I have neither father nor mother

307

nor brother nor sister. One day I will tell you some things that may make you pity me."

Gavin was again surprised, but more wounded than surprised. He loved St. Arnaud with the devoted affection of his nature, full of enthusiasm, and without having lost a single illusion; and to have St. Arnaud speak of himself as unloved and unloving cut him to the heart. He said nothing, and St. Arnaud's next words reassured him.

"That meeting in the snow was as fortunate for me as it was for you; it gave me interests, affections; for what I said just now meant that I was cut off from those natural ties that give life most of its charm. I have many comrades—what are called friends—but, except yourself, there is not one who feels very near to me. I do not know why it is so. I was ever ready to make friends, but I only know that you are the one person who knows my inmost thoughts, the one person to whom I can ever tell the story of my life."

"Well, then, tell it to me whenever you like," cried Gavin joyously. "And all I can say is, if you have an enemy, let him beware of me!"

The levee was exceptionally brilliant, and the event of the evening was undoubtedly the appearance together of Sir Gavin and Lady Ham-

ilton. Gavin, in a fever of excitement, pride, joy,
triumph, and nervousness, waited to see them enter the grand saloon where the Empress Queen and
Emperor received. Presently they were seen advancing—Lady Hamilton radiant in the beauty of
her youth, which seemed to have returned to her,
and Sir Gavin as cool and unconcerned as if a rec-
onciliation with his wife were no more than re-
joining her after a journey. Prince Kaunitz remarked confidentially to his intimate, the French
ambassador:

"What a loss, monsieur, to diplomacy is Sir
Gavin Hamilton! Observe his composure, and see
how he outwits all of his enemies by doing the
unexpected thing in the unexpected manner. I
understand he made no move to keep Lady Hamilton with him permanently until she informed him
she should leave his house immediately he performed this act of restitution; but as soon as he
found that out, he has been using all his endeavours
to make her stay. If she remains with him, she
can make her position entirely secure and agreeable
by occasionally offering to leave him. The rule of
Sir Gavin Hamilton's life is the rule of contrary."

By St. Arnaud's artful manœuvring, Gavin

found himself directly behind his father and mother when they made their obeisance to royalty. The Empress Queen, who knew the circumstances perfectly well, was peculiarly gracious to Lady Hamilton, as was the Emperor.

"Permit me to congratulate you upon your son, Lieutenant Hamilton," she said, with her charming smile and an air of imperial grace. "General Loudon has spoken of him to the Emperor and myself with great praise. It is to such young officers as he that we look for our safety and that of our children."

"My son ever considers it an honour to serve your Majesties," was Lady Hamilton's reply; and behind her was Gavin, blushing, confused, only half hearing the Empress Queen's kind words to him, but wholly happy.

At midnight, under a brilliant moon, Gavin and St. Arnaud stood together in the silent street before Sir Gavin Hamilton's splendid house. The great door was slightly ajar, and occasionally Lady Hamilton's figure passed in front of it.

"Go in," said St. Arnaud, in a quiet, determined voice. "Your father has asked you; your mother pleaded with you with her eyes. This is the turning-point. Go in for your mother's sake."

"Yes—for her sake," said Gavin after a moment. In that moment he had lived through the hardest struggle of his life.

St. Arnaud walked home alone—and for the first time Gavin Hamilton slept under his father's roof.

THE END.